Reasons of Hate

When Charles Hampton, returning from a spell with horses in the Gulf, found that his guardian had been murdered in Ireland, apparently in an abortive raid for arms, he little knew into what maze of violence, mystery and intrigue his appointment as executor to the estate was going to land him. An enigmatic warning of evil to come had been left him by his guardian and pursuit of the clues it contained led him to hairsbreadth escapes and hurried journeys which stretched from Ireland and Gloucestershire to the Blue Grass country of Kentucky and the Basses-Pyrénées.

His companion in these adventures is his guardian's daughter, Jo, as avid for the truth as he is. As love develops between them the reader is treated to some fascinating sidelights on the bloodstock industry and certain of its inhabitants, and learns of an old secret from the Second World War, kept but not forgotten.

As in his previous books, John Welcome keeps up the pace throughout, and his sense of place and knowledge of the world of which he writes make this an exciting, contemporary and compelling read.

by the same author

A PAINTED DEVIL

Novels

RUN FOR COVER
STOP AT NOTHING
WANTED FOR KILLING
GO FOR BROKE
GRAND NATIONAL
BELLARY BAY
A CALL TO ARMS

Biography

FRED ARCHER: HIS LIFE AND TIMES
NECK OR NOTHING:
THE EXTRAORDINARY LIFE AND TIMES OF BOB SIEVIER
THE SPORTING EMPRESS:
THE LOVE STORY OF ELIZABETH OF AUSTRIA AND BAY MIDDLETON
THE SPORTING WORLD OF ROBERT SURTEES

JOHN WELCOME

Reasons of Hate

COLLINS, 8 GRAFTON STREET, LONDON W1

William Collins Sons & Co. Ltd
London · Glasgow · Sydney · Auckland
Toronto · Johannesburg

First published 1990

British Library Cataloguing in Publication Data

Welcome, John
Reasons of hate.—(Crime Club)
I. Title
823'.914 [F]

ISBN 0 00 232299 4

Photoset in Linotron Baskerville by
Rowland Phototypesetting Ltd
Bury St Edmunds, Suffolk
Printed in Great Britain by
William Collins Sons & Co. Ltd, Glasgow

CHAPTER 1

'He wasn't killed by subversives, at least not the kind of subversives you're thinking of,' Jo Manners said, sitting with her firm little chin on her hands and staring at me across the room.

'What makes you say that?' I said.

'First, because the subversives always claim responsibility when they've committed a murder or an outrage, and this time they haven't.' She raised a hand and began ticking the reasons off on her fingers. 'Second, because they were discovered by Cassidy, the stud groom, who heard something and they bolted. If they'd been subversives I think they'd have stayed to shoot it out or at least tie him up while they got on with the job. Third, and most important, he was behaving strangely for a few weeks before it happened, as if he was on to something or—oh, I don't know—he was on edge.'

'Yes, but—' I said.

'Stop interrupting. You asked me a question and I'm trying to think out loud. I know they took the guns out of the gun-rack and got his keys and took the money out of the safe to make it look like a raid for money and arms. That's what the police—the Garda—think. But,' she added, with a defiant tilt of her chin, 'I still don't believe it.'

Jo Manners was my third cousin once removed or something of that sort, I never could work out these complicated relationships. Anyway, I'd been brought up with the family since my parents had been killed in an air crash when I was eight. Her father had been a regular soldier and after the war he had retired to the family home, Pollardstown House in Co. Kilderry, where he trained a few steeplechasers for himself and his friends as his father and grandfather had done before him. Pollardstown House—that was where I had spent my school holidays and my vacations from the University, growing up with Jo and her brother Mike, who had followed his father into the army and been killed in a tank accident in Germany a few years back. They'd been a united family who came even closer together after the death of the Colonel's wife and the children's mother when we were all in our teens.

I looked at Jo again. She had become a very attractive girl, I thought, since I'd been away, with her heart-shaped face and the sort of bloom to her complexion that seems to come to some girls brought up in the mists of the Irish midlands, and the sparkle in her eyes that some of them have, too. But her expression had not lost that touch of hardness, the determination to get what she wanted, the drive for the top, call it what you will, that I had known in her and her brother since we were children. Her eyes were now resting on me with a coolly appraising look.

I had just returned from two years in the Gulf and was living in a borrowed flat in Queen's Gate Gardens. I'd heard the news of the death of the Colonel (we all called him that) too late to attend the funeral, but I had written a long letter to send her my condolences and say how sorry I was. It was genuine enough, for I was fond of the old boy who had taken me in and was kind to me in his own way, despite the fact that he had been quite unable to hide his opinion that I was so wet I was pretty near useless and that had I had the misfortune to have been born earlier and sent to him as a subaltern, I'd have lasted about five minutes—flat.

Now here was his daughter sitting opposite me and saying she had come over specially to see me and propounding the most extraordinary notion about the Colonel's end. The whole incident, though tragic, had appeared straightforward enough from the few press reports I had read of it, and obviously the authorities thought so too.

There had been a raid on the house at night and the Colonel had either come down and disturbed the raiders, or had been sitting up late when they had broken in. Either way, being him, he had gone for them, been hit several times either by the butt of a revolver or by the traditional blunt instrument, and died.

'He had a weak heart, didn't he?' I said.

'Yes, and that's what killed him in the end. It's awful and I hate going back over this. He'd been beaten up a bit before he died, as if they'd been trying to get him to tell them something. Oh, if only Mike was alive—'

I've already said that the Colonel didn't think much of me, rather like one of his spaniels who was harmless enough to have around the place, but who didn't come up to scratch when it came to working under the guns. In fact, in that family, if I ever did manage to do something well one or the other would say either to me or to whoever happened to be standing by—'I never thought he had it in him' or some such. It didn't help, I suppose, being brought up with Mike and Jo. They were both stars in the pony club and on all the teams, whereas I invariably fell off or went the wrong course or otherwise made an ass of myself and was relegated to carrying buckets, horse-holding or helping with the saddling, which latter task I usually got wrong.

'You're nothing but a nothing, you're not a thing at all,' Mike and Jo used to chant at me when I had, in their eyes, made a more than usual mess of things with horse, rod or gun, but at the same time they did their best, in their offhand way, to initiate me into these mysteries. This was a line from a song, I think it came originally from *Snow White and the Seven Dwarfs*—which they had picked up and it gave me an idea. If I could merge myself into the background I was likely to be less likely to be noticed and therefore picked on. I adopted what might be called a protective non-colouring or, as I described it to myself, an ability to fade into the wainscotting. And it worked. No one expected anything of me, no one bothered me, and I watched and waited and picked things up as I went along.

I picked up quite a lot, as it happened, because behind the façade I was building I was determined to make myself into something where they couldn't sneer or jeer at me. Sooner or later I'd show them that I wasn't so wet you could shoot snipe off me, as I once heard Mike describe me to one of his pals. The fact that I was always given the worst ponies or, later, horses to ride if I was given anything at all in an odd way helped, too, because I had to try like hell to make something of them. I had another ally as well since Cassidy, the old stud groom, took pity on me and did all he could in his rough and ready way to teach me and to encourage me.

I remember once I got placed on a bad brute in a jumping competition when the others laughed and said it was a false result—Mike's pony had had one of his bad days and had had everything down—Cassidy came up to me and said, 'Stick to it, Master Charles, you'll show them all yet.' That put a bit of heart into me and I went on trying.

Also, I discovered books. Sometime in the last century Jo's grandfather, or perhaps great-grandfather, had built on an addition to the house. It was the fashionable thing to do among the Anglo-Irish at that time. The room in the new wing were the fashionable ones too, for it contained a library and a billiard room. The library was stocked with sets of the classics, reference books like Burke and Debrett and Baily's Hunting Directory. I don't know if the old boy ever read a book himself, I rather think not, for many of the volumes I found had their pages uncut. But I did. The library became my refuge and release from the loneliness of the rejected. When the others were out performing their prodigies in field sports and I wasn't wanted as an acolyte I would creep away there and, curled up in one of the big leather armchairs which smelled faintly of must, I would dream the days away with Quentin Durward or D'Artagnan, progressing later to Trollope, Thackeray and Dickens, whom I hated. There was also the heady poetry of Macaulay, Byron and Scott, much of which I learnt by heart, and I enjoyed 'Beating the Favourite' with Adam Lindsay Gordon—the only time I was likely to, incidentally, but I found myself even now repeating it over and over when sleep wouldn't come.

When the time came Mike went to Eton—of course—while I was packed off to one of the minor, tougher public schools. 'He's still a bit damp behind the ears,' I heard the Colonel explain to my housemaster when he delivered me there (I had faded into the background so successfully that neither realized I was within ear-shot). 'You may be able to bring him on a bit, harden him up.' I think he had an idea it might make a man of me. Well, it did, I suppose, but not in the way he expected. I continued to develop my protective non-colouring and this enabled me to dodge the worst of the bullying, and I wasn't good-looking enough to engage the homosexual attentions of the predatory rugger toughs.

In the course of time I arrived in the History Sixth. It was those books I'd read that got me there, helped by a sort of photographic memory for rollicking rhymes so that I was able to recite the whole of Macaulay's 'Naseby' to my amazed form-master. He became bored listening and it clinched my promotion. The school was anxious to get people into the older universities, and because the History Sixth was packed with athletes who had nowhere else to go if they were to escape superannuation and I was one of the few who could not only read and write but actually spell, my name was somehow put on to the list of those who would sit for Oxford entrance.

The Colonel, I am convinced, only permitted it to go forward because he was certain I had no hope of getting in. When the letter came telling him I had succeeded, he kept looking from it to me over his half-glasses and muttering, 'Extraordinary. Extraordinary. Didn't know you had it in you. Maybe after all you have some brains to make up for the rest.' I felt like saying that that was what occupied the wetness behind my ears, but I didn't.

At Oxford it was much the same. The reputation for wetness had preceded me from school, and I did nothing to dissipate it. I read history. I lived quietly and did very little work. No one seemed to want me to do more, for I kept my head down and got in nobody's way. I was lucky in that I went to tutorials with a man who had the name of being brilliant. He read my tutor long, learned essays, some studded with epigrams after the manner of Guedalla, others full of sly wit and outrageous suggestions—sort of Sub-A. J. P. Taylor stuff. My tutor was entranced and they would have long discussions on the Angevin Kings or the Ministry of All the Talents or some such things, while I dozed in a corner. Occasionally, five or ten minutes before the end, my tutor would wake up to the fact that I was there. 'My goodness, your essay,' he would say. 'Let's see, what was it? We haven't much time. Tell me about it. Next week you must read to me.' But next week the two of them would be off on the War of the Spanish Succession or Nelson's naval tactics at Trafalgar or some other piece of arcane historical interest.

In this way I succeeded in writing at the most two essays a term, leaving me lots of time to go to a trainer out Banbury way into whose care I had put myself with the object of learning how to sit a racehorse at speed and over fences, for I was still determined sometime to be able to hold my own with those cousins of mine. Once or twice I was nearly caught out at these tutorials, the closest call being when I read the same essay twice. Fortunately my tutor was not paying much attention and he accepted my explanation that I had left the current essay in my rooms by mistake, for he could never bring himself to believe that anyone who looked as blank and innocuous as I did could be actually trying to deceive him.

But at the beginning of my last year I realized that if I were not to go down without a degree I'd better do some work. I could imagine what the Colonel would say about feeding useless mouths if I ploughed, for his parting words to me before I went up, said with one of his smiles which took much of the sting out of them, had been, 'Since you don't seem to be able to do much else, you'd better put those brains of yours to work and we'll all be proud of you.'

I cut out the visits to the trainer, borrowed a set of notes from a friend, brewed black coffee and sat down and swotted. All the same, I was pretty terrified when Schools came round and I passed the interval before the results were announced in a cold sweat. I was in Oxford when they came through, and as I scanned the lists of fourths and thirds without finding my name among them, my heart dropped through my boots. In a sort of despair I lifted my eyes to higher things and saw my name where I could scarcely credit that it had any right to be, for I had got a second. It could hardly be a mistake, because there it was in cold print —*Second Class Honours. C. H. Hampton.* As I've said, I could scarcely believe it. Nor could my tutor. A little later I met him crossing the quad. He stopped and stared at me. 'Well,' he said. 'A second, I see. I felt there might be some mistake, but there isn't, it seems. And Bates' (this was the brilliant chap) 'only got a second too. I find it quite bewildering.'

'Well, you see, sir,' I said. 'I have a way of fading into the wainscotting.'

'Really,' he said. 'I understood only rats did that.' And he walked on. I thought that a bit uncalled for.

After Oxford, no one seemed to know what to do with me, least of all the Colonel, whose own children were pursuing their glamorous galloping careers with great success. Mike blossomed into a useful amateur rider, and Jo took up eventing; she had been on the Irish Junior International team and gone on from there to compete in open events. In the end, I went into a racing stable at Lambourn for a bit, as a sort of assistant to the assistant trainer. I learnt a lot one way or another, but here I rather over-played my hand in making myself inconspicuous, for after a few months the Guv'nor sent for me. 'I don't think you've quite got the personality for a racing stable,' he said. And that was that. Then I sort of drifted into a stud as general dogsbody. It wasn't much of an existence and I didn't care about the bloodstock world, its habits or its inhabitants. They're a fancy, flashy lot, and so far as I was concerned, you could have them all, and their money in telephone numbers too.

There was one of them I particularly disliked. He was a loud-mouthed bloodstock agent, a florid-looking chap called Francis Aloysius O'Shaughnessy, who threw his weight about as if he owned the place and everything in it. As a matter of fact, he did own a substantial share in two of the stallions, and also, in some way, had influence in positions in the sales catalogues. It was said of him, too, that if you crossed him, you were likely to have unwelcome visitors. So, by and large, no one dared tell him where to get off.

On his visits to the stud, which were quite frequent and made by helicopter, O'Shaughnessy's usual practice was to come into one of the yards shouting and roaring demands, instructions and commands to be waited upon by anyone who happened to be about, and flaying them with curses if they didn't jump to obey. I took good care to keep out of his way and to do my vanishing act when he was around.

But one morning I was unlucky. I went to the manager's office with a message and found him standing in front of the desk roaring like a bull about something as was his custom. A bottle of champagne, which he required to be ready for him on these visits as his mid-morning tipple, stood on a side table. He turned at my entrance, and, catching sight of me, shouted: 'Hey you! Open that bottle and be damn quick about it!'

Well, as I've said, I didn't much care about him, his habits or, for that matter, the clothes he wore. That morning he had on a flared tweed jacket in black and white checks about the size of a garden spade, and a shirt with shamrocks on it. There was a fashion just then for neckties with figures of nude women on them. He had selected the loudest and most explicit of them all and the various poses were mostly full frontal.

I opened the bottle, and of course, as was to be expected with me, since opening a bottle of champagne is a skilled business, I made a mess of it. But in fact I didn't make a mess of my aim. He had turned back towards the desk, ignoring me. The cork came out with a satisfactory crack like a pistol shot and, also like a pistol shot, flew exactly where I wanted. It got him plumb behind the right ear, and as the range was only a foot or so, I imagine it hurt. At all events, he leapt fully six inches off the floor, clapped his hand to the injured spot and the roar which exploded from him was the sort you'd expect from an outraged buffalo about to charge. I was afterwards told it was heard in the foaling yard fully quarter of a mile away. I think this was an exaggeration.

Anyway, I gasped in pretended horror, and of course the champagne continued to gush from the bottle. I can't deny that I helped its direction a bit with my thumb across its mouth so that it saturated the expansive seat of his beautiful

Bedford cord trousers, cut for him no doubt by Huntsman or Poole, or the best of the best at any rate. That put him in a bit of a fix for he didn't know which hand to put on which injury, with the result that he started to revolve like some vast top spinning and shouting at the same time. The only words I heard were: 'You clumsy, lousy little bastard. You useless—'

At this point I replaced the bottle on the side table and quietly faded away.

That afternoon I was summoned to the manager's office. I knew what was coming and made up my mind to forestall him. 'I'm sorry about this morning, sir,' I said. 'The bottle slipped in my hand.'

He looked at me as if he had never seen me before. 'Hm,' he said. 'It slipped in a remarkably accurate fashion, then. Mr O'Shaughnessy is not pleased. How long have you been here?'

'Six months,' I said.

'As long as that? Odd. I don't seem to have seen much of you. I have a feeling now that it might be better for us both if you looked for other and more suitable employment.'

'Yes, sir. When am I to go?'

'I wouldn't put it quite like that. I knew your guardian, Colonel Manners, in the army. Just look around for something, will you? And keep out of Mr O'Shaughnessy's way when he comes again.'

He must have written or got in touch with the Colonel, for a few days later an envelope addressed to me arrived from him, enclosing a cutting from *Sporting Life*. It was an advertisement stating that the Sheikh of one of the smaller Gulf States wanted an assistant to the man who was in charge of his racing and breeding interests. Clipped to the cutting was a postcard with the one word APPLY written on it, and underneath were the Colonel's scrawled initials.

So I applied, and to my astonishment was summoned to

an interview. When I went to tell the stud manager of this and to ask permission for an afternoon off to go to London for it, 'I know,' he said. 'I'm answering an inquiry about you.'

Just then he was summoned away to deal with some pressing matter. When he had left the room I went round the desk and glanced at what he had written. I had only time to read the last sentence before footsteps outside made me hastily return to my seat. '*Do not be deceived*,' it ran. '*He is not as harmless as he looks.*'

Whether it was this unorthodox recommendation, I don't know, but I got the job. Afterwards, I heard I was one of only three applicants because the Sheikh had the name of being both mean and tough and the salary offered, though it seemed magnificent to me, was little enough by oil-rich standards.

When I arrived, I found the reputation for toughness was well deserved. The Sheikh had a personal bodyguard commanded by an ex-SAS captain who also looked after the horses and the racing side and was my immediate boss. Every employee who was likely to come into contact with His Highness was required to undergo a commando-type course before taking up his duties so that he too could act as protector if need arose. When I heard this I nearly demanded my return ticket. I had some doubts about my ability to survive it because if you've been brought up as a poor relation, and a useless one at that, doubts tend to stick, but I was beginning to toughen myself behind the gormless façade I'd erected and so I took it on without protest. I hadn't much option really, for the SAS guy assured me if I didn't I'd probably be clapped into the slammer instanter for disobedience and linger there until the Sheikh decided what to do with me, the least of which would be to have my ears cut off before I was shipped home! As it happened, I almost enjoyed it and when the SAS guy said 'You'll do,' I felt I'd notched up another couple of points in my game against life, or perhaps I should say the Manners family.

As it fell out, I got on all right with the Sheikh despite all the hard things that had been said about him. I suppose the general sort of anonymity which I had preserved helped a bit here and he didn't take me too seriously, least of all as a threat. He was, as they said, more than a bit of a shit, but I liked him better than those bloodstock bastards I'd lately been mixing with, and if you took him right and laughed when he laughed (which wasn't often) and kept your lip buttoned at other times, he was amiable enough, and he was mad keen on his horses.

The contract was for two years, but after a year my immediate boss, the SAS captain, came into money from an aunt and decided to go home and look after it. The Sheikh asked me to take on his job at his salary, which I did, and when that year was out he suggested I should stay on. But by that time I'd had enough of the heat and the desert. I wanted to see green fields again. I'd been an expatriate too long and I had by now a nice chunk of sterling stashed away in the Isle of Man so I could afford to look around a bit.

When I came back I'd nowhere to live, but I had run into a chap I'd been at school with when having a drink in Jules' Bar. He was, of all things, an explorer and was just off on an expedition to the Andes or somewhere similar. His father had been a noted shikar in his day and had died a month or so back, leaving his flat and its contents to him. He suggested I borrow the flat and live there while he was away and I moved in.

It wasn't exactly cosy, for its walls were covered with trophies that had fallen to the shikar's gun. Bison, elk, buffalo, ovis poli and other unnamed species glared and leered at you from their mounts on the walls. There were tiger and leopard skins on the floor and a waste-paper basket made from an elephant's foot. In the little hallway, believe it or not, was a full-sized stuffed bear with a tray for visiting cards laid across his outstretched paws. He had, I was told, frightened the wits out of one or two of the shikar's unwary visitors, especially those who had been sampling his gin. Despite these ornaments, I liked it well enough; I had no fixed abode and it did as a base while I looked around.

I have put all this down in some detail because it helps to explain the attitude of my cousin and her father towards me and also a good deal of what was to happen and how it happened in the immediate future. But the little Jo had already said and her manner indicated that her opinion of me had not changed since my poor relation days, and why she had come to me now and what she wanted from me I could not imagine.

'I don't suppose,' I said to her, 'that you've travelled all the way from deepest Ireland to bury your woes in my manly breast. What's going on, Jo?'

She darted me a look that had precious little cousinly affection in it. 'He's made you the sole executor of his will,' she said.

'What? Sole executor? That means one is in charge of everything until the whole estate is wound up, doesn't it?'

'That's what the solicitor says.'

'Why in heaven's name did he do that?'

'Exactly. That's just what I'd like to know too. It was done, the new will, shortly before it—it happened, when he was behaving sort of strangely, like I said. He asked about you, if I'd heard from you and when were you due back from the Gulf, and that your contract must be just about up. He left you his desk, too. Here, I've got a copy of the will.' She opened her bag and took out two typewritten sheets of legal paper.

The will was a simple one. There were a few small bequests to members of the staff at Pollardstown. The residue went to Jo, and I was made sole executor. But it was the bequest to me which interested me. It read: *I give and bequeath 'the desk in my study' to my executor Charles Hampton.*

'Why did he put the words "the desk in my study" in inverted commas?' I asked her.

'Search me. He left you a letter too. It's marked "by hand of officer only" which means you'll have to come over and get it. The solicitor has it. The solicitor told me to tell you,' she went on, 'that you can renounce, I think that's the word, if you like. And of course we'll see that any expense you're put to will be paid.' She was looking at me speculatively as she spoke and at the back of that look I could see all the doubt I had seen so often before in the eyes of herself, her brother and her father.

I didn't care much about that look. I thought I'd had enough of it from her family. I was my own man now and I was tempted to tell her to go jump in the lake and take the will with her, but her next words and the open contempt they contained made me hesitate.

'I expect you will like,' she said. 'The solicitor drew up a form of renunciation for you to sign. I have it here.' Once more she opened her bag and took out a folded piece of paper. 'I can't imagine, knowing you, that you'll want to have anything further to do with it or us. Here it is. There's where you sign.' She pointed to a pencilled cross at the foot of the form.

'I'll have to think about it,' I said. 'Give me twenty-four hours and I'll let you know.'

That, I thought, would make her simmer for a bit, which wouldn't do her any harm at all. Besides, I did seriously want time to think about what I might be letting myself in for. It was true that I had no plans for the coming months, but on the other hand I wasn't at all sure I wanted to go back over old unhappinesses. On the other hand, the Colonel had asked my help. What on earth had made him appeal to the despised and rejected Charles Hampton and leave that mysterious letter in the solicitor's hands?

'Have you any idea what is in the letter and why the mystery about "by hand of officer"?' I asked her.

'None whatever. He was always one for a bit of mumbo-jumbo, as perhaps you remember. He was in one of those funny services towards the end of the war. SOE—Special Operations Executive or something, I think it was called. That seemed to have given him a taste for secrecy and ciphers and that sort of thing.' She sighed. 'I really know damn-all about it.'

'SOE,' I said. 'I didn't know that.' Growing up, I had never thought about the Colonel's army career. He had always seemed a remote sort of godlike figure to me, far older of course and Olympian in a sort of way. I knew he had been decorated somewhere, in the desert I think, but apart from that if I'd considered it at all I'd have imagined him to be a straightforward, straight bat fighting soldier. Now, it seemed, he was a bit different.

'I didn't know anything about the cloak and dagger stuff until Mike was killed,' she said. 'We became very close after that. He missed Mike dreadfully and he used to talk to me about him and his hopes for him and about the horses. We used to plan their programmes together, not that any of them were much good, worse luck. He didn't talk much about the war but he did let drop that something happened in the desert after he got that immediate DSO. He came home then and got into SOE. I remember him saying that life was full of dirty tricks, that life caught up with you. He hinted that he had stumbled on something and was wondering just what he should do. Could it have been something to do with that time when he was dropped into France? I just don't know. It's all so long ago—another world. Well, what are you going to do, Charles?'

'I'll tell you after twenty-four hours,' I said.

She looked at me with that flash of the old devil where I was concerned coming back into her eyes, together with that look of exasperation I knew so well. I couldn't resist the temptation to tease her a bit. 'Go ahead,' I said. 'Stamp your foot. Say "fiddle-de-dee" like Scarlett O'Hara in *Gone With The Wind.*'

'No one could mistake you for Rhett Butler, that's for sure. Did she really say that?'

'I shouldn't think so. I never read the immortal tome. I saw it on the box. Did you know Ingrid Bergman never said "play it again, Sam"?'

'No, and I'm beginning not to know what this conversation is about. You always go off on tangents. It's that bloody business of your being up at Oxford. You think yourself damn clever, don't you?'

'I scarcely think a knowledge of *Gone With The Wind* and *Casablanca* would get you a first in Eng. Lit.' I was annoying her and I knew it and in a mean way I was enjoying it. My having got into Oxford always rankled with them and touched a sore spot.

'Oh, you're impossible—'

'Go on, say it—fiddle-de-dee. Shall I spell it for you?'

Suddenly she laughed and gave me one of those quick, dazzling smiles which reminded me of her father. One thing about that family, they let fly at you and then forgot it. 'All right,' she said. 'You win. Twenty-four hours. I'm staying with an aunt in Clapham. Give me a piece of paper and I'll write her number down.'

I tore a sheet from the pad by the telephone. She scribbled on it and handed it back to me. As she did so she looked at me again. 'You've changed, Charles,' she said. 'Those desert sands have done something for you.'

'They were red with the wreck of a square that broke,' I said. 'And I learnt how to play up, play up and play the game.'

'That's something you never did at home.' She stood up and smoothed down her skirt. 'I'll be getting back to Aunt Miriam.' Then for the first time she appeared to become aware of her surroundings and looked about her. 'Good heavens, what a place,' she said. 'It's too much to hope you killed all those on your travels, I suppose?'

'No,' I said. 'The Gatling jammed before I got to them.'

'What in hell is a Gatling?'

'Something like that only bigger—' I pointed to where a Frontier Colt which had been given to the shikar on one of his excursions to the American West now lay as a strange sort of bibelot along with its accoutrements on plush velvet in an inlaid ebony box. 'One of the early Colts,' I said. 'It's so heavy and unwieldy I can scarcely lift it, let alone use it. Yet Wyatt Earp and Co. would try to shoot flies off the ends of each others' noses with it.'

'But of course,' she said sweetly, looking me squarely in the eye in the way she had. 'After all, they were men in those days, weren't they?'

I couldn't help laughing as I closed the door of the lift behind her. She'd had the last word and won the last round, but that was a way she had, too.

CHAPTER 2

As it happened, I had a lunch date. It was with Denzil Colton, ex-SAS, who had been my boss with the Sheikh and who was now enjoying his inheritance and making a bit extra in freelance racing journalism. He took me to Overton's and over avocados, sole Véronique and a pricey bottle of Montrachet he told me he was liking his new life, he had plenty of contacts, and although the money he made wasn't great it paid his drink bill or very nearly.

I asked him the question which was uppermost in my mind after the interview with Jo. 'What, if anything, do you know about SOE?' I said.

'My father was one of them for a bit,' he said, surprisingly. 'Until he got fed up and got out. Some regular soldiers didn't fit in and he was one of them. I never knew quite how he managed it, because once in they didn't like letting you go. "They were a strange lot," he always said. Why do you ask?'

'A friend of mine has been murdered in Ireland, my guardian as a matter of fact. The authorities say it was done by subversives raiding for arms and that he got in the way. His daughter, who is the only one of the family left, doesn't accept the official line. It's too easy a way out and there are other things against it too. She believes it may hark back to his SOE days, that there may have been some cloak and dagger element in it. I'm supposed to be the executor. It may be all nonsense, probably is, but he's left me some sort of sealed message, "by hand of officer only," so perhaps there is some connection. I thought I should at least chase up that line of inquiry. Is your father likely to know anything of him?'

He pursed his lips. 'It's a long time ago,' he said. 'What was your guardian's name?'

'Lieutenant-Colonel Manners, DSO, MC,' I said.

'I'll ask my father to see if he remembers anything of him. But it was all pretty secretive even inside the operation from what I've gathered. Not let the left hand know what the right was doing sort of thing. And Father is old now and his memory isn't too good. Anyway, just what is it you want to know?'

'That's the bugger,' I said. 'It's all so vague. Anything at all he could come up with, I suppose. All I can tell you is that he was on edge before it happened and he seems to have hinted that it came from the past—the war.'

'It's vague all right. I wouldn't count on anything coming from it,' he said. 'Where can I reach you?'

I gave him the telephone number of the flat and then added, 'If I'm not there I might be in Ireland,' and scribbled the Pollardstown address on the back of an envelope.

We lingered over brandies talking about our times in the desert and when we poured ourselves out into St James's Street I thought I might as well spend some of my new-found wealth in buying a few decent shirts to replace the tropical kit needed in the Gulf. That took a bit of time and one way or another it was latish in the afternoon when I returned to the flat.

I was turning over the events of the day in my mind as I put my key into the lock on the outer door and entered the hallway. The lift was waiting and empty and I stepped in. I was about to close the door when someone joined me. I assumed that the lift had just come down and he had been waiting for it and, still preoccupied with my own thoughts, I didn't pay much attention to him. 'Third floor,' I said as I reached for the control button.

'That'll do me,' he said.

I did look at him then. He was a huge man with a tiny head and a tweed hat pulled down over it so that I really could not see much of his face. He didn't speak again but stared at the walls of the lift. When it came to a halt I got out and opened the door of the flat. He had followed me and as I turned the key I did switch my thoughts to wonder what the hell he was doing there. It was too late.

A fist the size of a ham took me under the ribs. It felt as if my whole ribcage had been smashed in by a pile-driver. It also hurt like hell. I folded up. Then two great arms like those of an outsize orang-outang went round me, pinioning me, and I was lifted bodily into the flat. I was helpless. What little knowledge of unarmed combat I had learned was no use to me, for I was caught in a grip like a steel band, handled like a toy, breathing hard and in pain.

It was Bruin, the bear, who saved me. The hallway was narrow and dark; he stood at an angle, facing the door and not three feet away from where we were. As I've mentioned, I'd been warned that he'd put the fear of God into several of my predecessor's visitors. He did it again now, bless him.

The gorilla who had me in his grip found himself staring over my shoulder straight at him. He must have thought, if he thought at all, that he'd blundered into an indoor safari park. I heard a sound something like 'Cor!' coming from him, and his grip loosened. In fact he pushed me away to deal with this new threat. That was his mistake.

I grabbed a knobkerrie from the wall and swung it as hard as I could at the back of his head. He was still half turning to look at the bear and the blow didn't land quite right. He shook his head as if a fly had brushed it, said something that didn't sound in the least like 'Cor!' and came after me again. His head was bent like a bull about to charge and that was his second mistake.

It was a real knobkerrie, the genuine article with a bloody great aboriginal rock in it covered with leather at the end of a long stick. I gave him another sixpenny one with it and this time I connected. His hat, which flew off, must have saved him a bit and I suppose there was nothing but sheer bone between his ears. He didn't go down right away as I had hoped but his knees began to buckle and it gave me time to bolt for the living-room.

The Frontier Colt was lying handy in its box and I grabbed it. He was still on his feet but only just and he moved like a man in his sleep. Getting both hands on the butt of the big revolver, I pointed it in his general direction. My thumbs felt for and found the hammer and it came back with a loud and satisfactory click. This penetrated to him, for he stopped in his tracks.

'Stay where you are,' I said, 'or I'll blast your stomach through your backbone.'

'Listen, guv,' he said shakily, 'I mean you no harm.'

'You've a quaint way of showing it, then,' I said. I had to keep him frightened so that he wouldn't get round to guessing the damn thing wasn't loaded. 'Listen to me. I can still blow a hole in your guts and get away with it as self-defence. Who sent you?'

'A geezer I met in a pub. Honest, guv. Fifty nicker 'e gave me. Said just to rough you up a bit. I didn't mean you no real 'arm.'

'Tell that to my ribs. They're still aching. What was his name?'

'I don't know. Please, guv, put that shooter down. It might go off.'

'That's the general idea. If it does you'll be the first to know.' He was probably telling the truth, I thought. He was in no condition and anyway hadn't the brains to make up a story at short notice.

'Did he say anything else?' I asked him.

'Blimey. I dunno. Will you put that shooter down, guv. I can't think like with it in me face.'

'I might when your memory comes back.'

His brow, what there was of it, for I now noticed it went straight back from his eyebrows to form a sort of plateau on the top of his head, furrowed, if that's the word, in whatever passed for thought inside it. He put his hand to his head and moved it back and forth a bit. 'What d'yer hit me with?' he said. 'A bloomin' sledge-hammer?'

'Something like that,' I told him. 'This thing is cocked and my trigger finger is getting tired. Come on. What did he say?'

'"Yerp," he said, belching quietly. '"Tell 'im," 'e said, "to go back to the desert. It's 'ealthier there." Swelp me, guv, those were 'is very words.'

'Did he then. What was he like, this geezer?'

'Big geezer, 'e was. He had a coat on 'im wiv checks on it like soup plates.'

'Well, if you see him again,' I said, 'tell him I'll be waiting for him with this cannon. Now, get out.'

'You're not going to hand me over to Old Bill? Thanks, guv.' He lumbered off towards the door, giving the bear a scary look as he went. I followed him with the Colt pointing to the small of his back just to keep him up to his word, and watched the door click shut behind him. Then I put the chain on the lock, patted the bear gratefully on the head and went back to the living-room. Lowering the hammer on the Colt, I returned it to its case. My ribs were still hurting like hell, reaction was setting in and I needed a drink. Crossing to the wig-box where the drinks were kept I opened it.

Pouring myself a stiff whisky, I sat down. After what had just happened, the assault on me with the obvious intention of frightening me off, what Jo had told me of her doubts and fears began to make more sense. I was beginning to ache. It hurt and I didn't like it. I didn't much care either about the casual way whoever was behind all this had estimated what it was worth to get rid of me. Fifty pounds was apparently my value. That brought back nasty memories. I poured myself another drink. Fifty pounds. Well, we'd see about that. I crossed to the telephone and punched out the number Jo had given me. 'I'll call for you at seven tomorrow morning,' I said to her, 'and drive you to the Fishguard boat.'

CHAPTER 3

There is a maze of streets beyond Clapham Common and of course I got lost and that meant I was late trying to find the address Jo had given me. She was waiting for me and she was not best pleased.

'I might have guessed you'd lose your way somehow,' she said. 'I should have given you a map, though even if I had I imagine you'd have read it wrong. Well, we'll just have to hurry—oh!'

The last exclamation was caused by the fact that she had caught sight of my car. Out of my newfound wealth I had bought myself a Porsche. I'd never had anything but old bangers before and I'd always hungered after a decent car, especially when I'd been at the stud and seen all those glossy people rolling up in their exotic models. I don't know why I picked on a Porsche except that it looked exciting and went like hell and so I bought it. After I had taken delivery I rather regretted it, since I learnt that while I had been away it had become the smart and fashionable conveyance for the up-coming with new money and I had no wish to be taken for one of those. Also I had to admit that sometimes when I put my foot down I felt rather as I did when Mike out of devilment put me up on one of his saucier rides which I couldn't either start or stop—over-horsed, in fact. But still it was fun to have.

'Can you control that slinky thing?' she said as she looked at it. 'I should have thought something a bit slower and staider would be more in your line.'

My ribs were still hurting and I'd spent a rotten night. 'With a bulb horn, acetylene lamps and room for a top hat inside to go to Ascot in,' I said. 'I tried for one but they've gone off the market. Get in for Christ's sake and we'll see what happens.'

'Would you like me to drive?' she said sweetly as she opened the car door. 'I do know the way.'

'You can tell it me as we go and give me instructions in good time,' I said. 'No, I don't want you to drive. This thing takes a bit of a hold. You'd be rather over-horsed.'

She didn't like that much and she liked it less when we

made the motorway and I gave the Porsche her head in the fast lane. The needle went up over the hundred and stayed there. She wasn't enjoying it one bit and I knew why. She still saw me as the nothing but a nothing she had so often scorned in our schooldays, who couldn't shoot or ride and had no business to be hurtling along at this lethal speed in this totally unsuitable vehicle. Stealing a glance at her out of the corner of my eye, I saw her pass a hand over the back of her head in a manner I'd observed men doing before they jumped out of aeroplanes over the desert. I smiled to myself and didn't break the silence which had fallen between us.

At length she said, almost meekly, I observed with some pleasure, 'Do you think we could stop for coffee at Severn Bridge? We seem to have made up some time.'

'Of course,' I said. 'I've been putting her along a bit. Shall I ease off? I'd hate to get your knickers in a twist.'

'You won't. And stop showing off, Charles. But if it's any comfort to you to know, I don't much care about being driven too fast by drivers I don't trust.'

'Thanks,' I said, and put my foot down again, swept past a line of lorries and watched the needle climb.

Inside the cafeteria we fetched our coffees and as she stirred hers I saw her regarding me as if I were a stranger. What she said after a moment or two surprised me. 'I suppose you think we were pretty bloody to you when we were growing up,' she said.

'That's right,' I said. 'I did, and I do.'

'You've changed, though. I said that yesterday. Do you still hate us all that much?'

It wasn't a question I was prepared to answer, at least not just then. I hadn't told her about the assault on me last evening and had not decided when I would, if at all. I wanted to see what was in that letter of the Colonel's before finally deciding on my course of action. 'Were you in the house the night he was killed?' I asked her.

'No. I was on a two-day dressage course at Borris, and thinking back, he was anxious that I should go to it when I mentioned it to him. And that's a bit odd, too. He never took much interest in eventing, dressage especially. He said it made a decent animal into a circus performer.'

'He wasn't far wrong.'

'You would say that. I don't recall you were any great shakes across a country yourself to enable you to swear at dressage.'

'I never had much under me, did I? You and Mike had the best. I had the screws and the scrubbers, which you'll also recall as your memory is so good.'

'There you are, I knew you hated us.'

'Who started this argument?'

'You did with your snide remark about dressage.'

'All right. As usual, you win. Let's go back to basics, shall we? Why did he want you to go?'

'I don't know, I told you. He was always secretive and he'd become more so in those last few weeks. I have a feeling, though, that he was expecting someone.'

'Had he any enemies?'

'None that I know of, unless you count the new people who are running racing now. Money barons who think of nothing else, he and his chum Bilby Barrows used to call them, and great times they had growling into their whiskies about them.'

'Bilby Barrows. I remember him. He was senior steward at one time, wasn't he? Used to go like a scalded cat out hunting. I suppose he's past it now.'

'He didn't come to the funeral. He was laid up with sciatica. When he wrote he did say, though, that he had had a strange letter from the Colonel shortly before and that the Colonel wanted to see him and did I know what it was all about.'

'So something was worrying him, but he was on good terms with everyone so far as you know?'

'That's right. The country people always liked him. There aren't many neighbours any more but those there are he got on with well enough. Even the new people who have come to Craddockscourt.'

'It's sold, is it?'

'Hadn't you heard? I suppose not, in the desert. Dick Willoughby got rid of a million or something like it double quick in the stud there through sheer stupidity, the Colonel used to say, and he had to sell up. An American tycoon called Amory Brayne bought it and moved in. The Colonel rather took to him. He's a quiet American, he used to say. He hasn't been around much since it—it happened. I'll have to sell the horses, or some of them anyway, I suppose. He might be in the market. Will I have to sell up, Charles?'

'I don't know,' I said truthfully. 'There was always money about, wasn't there?'

'That's what we thought but I wonder. Lately he'd been saying he was pulling the Devil by the tail—that was another of his expressions. I lie awake thinking what's going to happen. I wonder would Amory buy it and leave me there or something?'

'We'll have to see,' I said guardedly.

'Let's get on, then, it's time we weren't here, or are you going to break a few more records? The motorway hasn't reached Fishguard yet in case you didn't know.'

The Fishguard–Rosslare boat was on time and nearly empty. We were off and away through a flat calm sea arriving without any hassle or delay, and then drove through the Irish countryside where the grass glowed greener than on the other side of the water and the blue mountains lazed in the background. We had grills in a pub and the light was beginning to fail when we came to Pollardstown. It was a long, low, typical Irish Georgian house of two storeys set on a slight eminence which enabled its tall windows to look away to the far-off hills, and despite all that had happened there I never returned to it without the slight warm feeling of coming home.

'You can have your old room,' she said. 'Do you want coffee or a drink or anything? There's whisky on the grog tray.'

'Not particularly,' I said and, taking my bag, went up the well-remembered stairs lined with Snaffles and Lionel Edwards prints, and crossed the landing to my room. It was in the return, not quite in the servants' quarters but not in the main house where the family and guests slept, either. I put the bag on the bed, and, with memories crowding in on me, went over to the window, wondering why I had come. The light was fading quickly now and darkness was creeping across the fields and paddocks where young stock grazed. I had forgotten the almost perceptible stillness which comes with nightfall in the heart of the Irish countryside. As I stood there watching the shadows turn into night, it all brought back to me my long unhappy childhood and the times I had spent alone in that room envying my happier, healthier, more successful cousins and eating my heart out at my own failures. They say you never recover from an unhappy childhood. Maybe I hadn't, maybe I hadn't tried hard enough, or maybe it is true that you never do escape from it. Involuntarily I shivered, turned back into the room and switched on the light.

Nothing had been changed since I left it; still on the walls were the few Medici prints I had collected and defiantly hung there in opposition to the racing and hunting pictures of moving incidents by flood and field which proliferated elsewhere in the house. And then something caught my eye. Propped on the mantelshelf was the postcard print of Toulouse-Lautrec's *Le Jockey* which had not been there when I went away and I vividly remembered the occasion of its removal.

A friend from Oxford had sent it to me with the scrawled message on the back: *You in one of your lighter moments, I presume.* I had liked it and had placed it prominently on the mantelshelf where I could look at it. One evening a little later Mike, having nothing better to do, had wandered into the room where I was trying to do some work for my finals. The postcard had immediately caught his eye.

'What's this?' he said, picking it up.

'It's a racehorse and jockey in case you didn't know,' I said.

'I wouldn't have known if you hadn't told me. Damned odd-looking horse. Who drew it?'

'Toulouse-Lautrec. He's an Impressionist. One of the best.'

'What are the others like? That's a bloody silly name, I must say. I thought Toulouse was a town somewhere in Frogland. What age is he? About six? Look at those hocks. You could drive a cab between them.'

'What sort of a cab had you in mind—a hansom or a four-wheeler? Would you drive it yourself or get someone else?'

'You think yourself bloody clever, young Charles, don't you, just because you managed to get into Oxford. Well, I'll show you what I think of Mr Toulouse Longarse or whatever he's called. Can't have that sort of thing in this house.' He leant over my shoulder, took the card and tore it in half. Placing the pieces in the pocket of his rakish and well-cut riding jacket, he sauntered out of the room.

The whole little scene coming back vividly to my mind and stirring other memories, I picked up the card. Then a sound from the doorway made me look up. Jo was standing there watching me, her eyes on the card.

'I rang Mrs Connolly to tell her to put a hot bottle in your bed,' she said. 'We haven't run to electric blankets in all rooms yet. Have you got everything?'

'I expect so. Where did this come from?' I gestured with the card I held in my hand.

'Mike told me what he'd done,' she said. 'He thought it funny but I thought it pretty bloody. I knew you liked it so I looked in his waste-paper basket for it and taped it up. I put it there for you if you ever came back.'

This was a side of her I'd never seen before and I didn't know what to say. 'Well, thanks,' was all I could manage.

She took a step further into the room, seemed about to say something, hesitated and then changed her mind. 'Good night,' she said. 'Sleep well. Don't dream too much about old times.' She turned, went out and closed the door behind her.

I was left still staring at the card. Turning it over I saw how the pieces had been bound together with Sellotape. Putting it back on the mantelshelf from which Mike had rudely raped it, I thought about what she had done and why she had done it. Just possibly it seemed that someone in this house had a heart after all.

CHAPTER 4

Birdsong woke me next morning. Outside the window the sun was shining and apart from the birds the stillness held. Rather to my surprise, I had slept well and dreamlessly and I lay on for a bit thinking of what I had to do. I was pretty sure now that I would take on the task which the Colonel had allotted me and, however much she disliked the thought of it, I was sure, too, that Jo needed me. As well, I was by this time definitely sharing her doubts about the official verdict on the Colonel's death. When she had told me of them first I had been very much inclined to dismiss them as fantasies which come with the trauma of a sudden and violent death. But after the events of yesterday I was far from sure that I had been right. That the attempt to frighten me off was no simple mugging for money had been proved by the message the thug had been told to convey to me. It had been a mistake. I was a big boy now and had learnt to look after myself.

I must see Cassidy, the stud groom, for it was he who had disturbed the intruders whoever they were, but that would have to wait until I had interviewed the solicitor and read that mysterious letter which the Colonel had left for me and for that matter find out from him, if he'd tell me, whether he shared Jo's doubts about who had caused his death and why.

All these thoughts were in my mind as I went towards the head of the stairs. On my way I passed Jo's room. The door was open and she was inside bending over her dressing-table. She was wearing a loose dressing-gown and her hair was still damp from the shower. 'Hi!' she said, straightening up. 'Lazy old thing, aren't you? I've had two horses out already.' As she turned towards me the dressing-gown flew open. There was nothing underneath and I had a glimpse of a slim, taut body and high, proud breasts. 'Damn,' she said, grabbing the folds about her.

'That's all right,' I said. 'I know what little girls are made of. And very nice too, if I may say so.'

'Get along with you. Breakfast in the kitchen. I'll be down in a minute.'

I went on towards the stairs. I noticed now, in daylight, that there was a slight air of shabbiness over everything. The carpet had worn threadbare in places in the way carpets do and the mounts of the prints were speckled and stained; the paint on the wall behind them was cracked and peeling in places. Perhaps it had always been like that and I had not noticed, but now, fresh from the luxuries of the Gulf, it hit the eye. I remembered too, how, looking out the window the night before, I had noticed many of the stud rails had been broken and the gaps roughly patched.

They had turned the morning-room into a kitchen to save the trudge from the labyrinthine depths where the old one had lurked in a maze of sculleries and the usual offices. It was bright and airy with an Aga where the fireplace had been. There was an extension telephone on the wall and it was from there that I rang the solicitor. He would see me, he said, as soon as I cared to come in.

'Paul Davey,' Jo said in answer to my query about him. 'He and his firm have always looked after our affairs. You'll find him helpful though I don't like to think about what he'll tell of how things stand with the bank—if he knows.'

The solicitor's office in Kilderry, the county town, proved to be a square Georgian building set between two modern steel and concrete blocks—the new Ireland engulfing the old, I thought inconsequentially, and wondered what Davey himself would be like. There was a brass plate on the door with *Mr Davey's Offices* inscribed on it in barely decipherable letters which had been all but rubbed away by generations of polishing. I was not kept waiting and was shown almost immediately into his inner office.

He was sitting behind a large mahogany desk and, extending his hand, rose to greet me. As I took it I looked about me. There were tall windows overlooking the street, an octagonal rent table beside the desk, a Regency bookcase and a stack of deed boxes with white-painted family names on them along one wall. It was all orderly, neat and a trifle old-fashioned. He caught my glance and smiled. 'Marcus Davey and Sons,' he said. 'Servants of the Ascendancy for two hundred years, and now that there is no Ascendancy left still trying to catch up with the times.' He had the slightly amused air of a detached observer of human frailties and I felt instinctively that I could trust him.

'This is a sad business,' he went on as he motioned me to a chair.

'It is,' I said. 'I was brought up with them, but I'm sure you know that. I'm some sort of a cousin. I've never worked out the exact relationship . . .'

'You've read the will? I gave Jo a copy.'

'She showed it to me. Have you any idea why he made me his executor?'

'None at all. He wasn't an easy man to communicate with and he didn't care to be questioned. In the words of the Bible, he said do and thou doest, go and thou goest, and that was it. It was only about a week before it happened that he made the will.'

'And I gather he left a letter for me.'

'"By hand of officer only". I suppose I was the nearest thing to an officer he could think of in the time. I have it here.' He crossed to a safe in the corner, took out an envelope and handed it to me.

With a little pang I recognized the familiar scrawled handwriting in the address *Charles Hampton Esq.*, and sure enough written across the top were the words *By hand of officer only*. The envelope was sealed with the Colonel's seal, I noticed as I took the paperknife the solicitor handed me. Sealing is unusual to say the least in this day and age. He must have regarded whatever the message the letter contained as of special importance to go to that trouble. Idly I wondered where he had found the sealing wax. With a sense of anticipation I took the folded sheet of paper out of the envelope, but the letter it contained was brief enough.

My dear Charles [it ran],

Jo tells me you are due back from the Gulf. If you receive this letter you will know that something has happened to me. I have discovered something from the past or I think I have. I always felt that somewhere inside you was something more than we had troubled to find out. You once said you owed me a debt for what I had done for you. I am now calling in that debt. But you may, as you are perfectly entitled to do, refuse to pay it. If so, hand this letter back to Davey and see that he burns it unread. If, however, you decide to act as my executor, and you may trust Jo implicitly and consult her on everything, then consider carefully my bequest to you and what it contains. Use what none of us ever had a great deal of and we never thought you had either until you got that Oxford degree—your brains, my boy.

Your old friend,
R. C. T. Manners (Lt-Col. Retd)

I read the letter once more. If only he hadn't been so damn mysterious! But I thought I knew the reason for his clouding the issue this time. He suspected that I might run away from whatever had happened and renounce the executorship, as indeed I might have done if it hadn't been for that attempt to frighten me in the flat. If I were to renounce, then he didn't want to commit himself and whatever he knew to paper. That was reasonable enough. After all, he'd never thought much of me and he had no idea what I'd be like on my return from the Gulf. Folding the letter, I returned it to the envelope.

'I'm afraid I can't tell you what is in this,' I said as I put it into my pocket. 'It's a personal matter or so it seems to me.'

'Of course. I quite understand. I should tell you, though, that Colonel Manners asked me if the appointment of an executor was binding on the appointee and I told him it was not. You may renounce now if you so wish.'

'I've gathered that both from the letter and from what Jo told me. I've made up my mind. I won't renounce.'

'I'm glad. Jo will need all the help she can get.'

'Have you any idea why he put the bequest of the desk to me in inverted commas?'

'None whatever save that he insisted. I could only assume it was to stress its importance or to convey some sort of message. He was not an easy man to advise, as I've said. "I'm not here to be cross-examined. Save that for the courts," he told me on another occasion.' He smiled at the recollection.

'I can almost hear him saying it,' I said. 'One more question, or rather two. Jo tells me that the official version is that he was killed by subversives in a raid for arms. Are you satisfied that is correct?'

'The authorities are,' he said guardedly. 'As for myself, to be candid, I am not so sure. He was obviously worried and yes, apprehensive, I suppose you could say, when he made that will. I've seen the Garda superintendent. He accepts the subversive theory. There's a lot of crime in this town. He's a very busy man. He told me the thinking is that the perpetrators are now far away, well holed up in safe houses in Dundalk or Donegal.'

'And that's it, is it?'

'I'm afraid so.' He looked at me evenly. 'There's a lot of ambivalence in this country, Mr Hampton. Colonel Manners's coat was of the wrong colour, as to a certain extent mine is too. We go to the wrong churches, we were educated at the wrong schools. We pull no strings and wield no influence. We're survivors of a hated régime and some of that hatred lingers on, fanned, I'm sorry to say, by flames from the North. The case is closed.'

'Has there been an inquest.'

'There has, but that put it no farther. Unlike England where an inquest incorporates an inquiry, here it is confined to ascertaining the cause of death.'

'It seems to me, then, that you share some of Jo's doubts about the official version.'

'I'll put it this way. He was a worried man and the raid, if it was one, appears to me to have been too much of a coincidence. Next, raids for arms from private houses are, by and large, a thing of the past. Subversives now have plenty of sophisticated weaponry from the gallant colonel in Libya and elsewhere to concern themselves with going after a couple of twelve-bores in a private house. Finally, there was the sudden appointment of you as executor and although I don't know what is in it I have a shrewd suspicion that letter tells you something of what his fears concerned.'

'Did anyone know of my appointment?' I asked him, my bruises reminding me of my encounter with the thug in London.

'Not from me, though for all I know Jo may have told her friends. There have been several inquiries about the will and the estate, most of them, I'm sorry to say, from creditors.'

'That brings me to question two,' I said. 'What about the estate? Will there be anything left?'

He sighed. 'Not very much, I'm afraid,' he said. 'The bank holds the deeds of Pollardstown and he had borrowed heavily against them. The bank had been pressing him for some time, demanding that he either sell or reduce the debt. There are other, personal debts too. There is a small marriage settlement. Jo will get what is left of that but it won't amount to much. There were powers of advancement and he had raided it to pay for Mike's fees at Eton.'

'So the place will have to be sold?'

'It is too early to say but it looks very much like it. And with the recession here places are not too easy to sell. It may drag on, and frankly I don't see where the cash to carry on is coming from.'

Back in the street again I fetched the Porsche from the car park and drove to Pollardstown in a thoughtful mood. Turning into the stableyard, I went in search of Cassidy.

The stableyard at Pollardstown was built on a lavish

scale, making it far grander than the house. The Colonel's grandfather who built the new wing had pulled down the old stabling and erected boxes, tack rooms and grooms' quarters of cut stone round four sides of a square with an archway at either end. It was a typical piece of Victorian Ascendancy extravagance carried out before the Land Acts and the loss of their rent rolls had made such embellishments an embarrassment to their builders' descendants. The old boy had, I supposed, some excuse for his *folie de grandeur* since he had trained his horses here with considerable success. Though he had never won it, he had had horses placed in the National when it was the be-all and end-all of steeplechasing and the Conyngham Cup at Punchestown had decorated his sideboard on several occasions. Now only one range of boxes was kept up. The rest were empty or used as stores or boarding places for fowl.

I found Cassidy looking over the half-door of one of the boxes, gloomily contemplating its occupant. 'Makes a noise ye could hear in the next parish,' he observed to no one in particular. 'I told her he was too big to stay sound but she would buy him and when she gets a likin' for one 'tis the Divil himself wouldn't stop her.' And then, catching sight of me. 'Glory be to God, 'tis you, Master Charles, and 'tis good to see ye. There'll be a man about the place again now.'

'If you call me a man,' I said. 'Some of the people round here never did.'

'Arrah, go on wid ye. You was always belittlin' yourself. I used to tell ye that when ye were a chap. How are ye now, Master Charles?'

'Never better, if it wasn't for this terrible business about the Colonel. You found him, I think. Can you tell me what happened?'

'Bedad I can, for I'm not likely to forget it. Since the wife died I don't sleep as well as I might. And the times that are in it I goes around nights to see there's none of them thievin' blackguards that are about these days now tamperin' with the horses.'

That night, he went on, at some time past midnight, he saw a light in the Colonel's office, which was unusual for the Colonel kept early hours. Thinking something was wrong, he let himself in by a side door of which he had a key. As he did so he heard voices from the office. Either his footsteps on the flagged passage or else the noise he had made opening the door disturbed the intruders, for the sound of voices was suddenly hushed. Then came the slamming of a door and a car started up. In the office he had found the Colonel slumped in his chair, unconscious, purple in the face and scarcely breathing. He had phoned the doctor but 'the poor man expired' before he came.

I asked him had he seen or could he remember anything about the car in which the intruders had got away. No, he said, he had been too busy attending to the Colonel. Then I asked a question I should have put to him before. Had he found any signs of a break-in? No, he hadn't, and so far as he knew the Garda hadn't either. That meant, or at least my guess was that it meant, that the Colonel had gone to answer the door himself and let the intruders in. So it looked as if he was expecting someone. And it was clear from the voices Cassidy had heard that there had been more than one. So I had learnt something, if not very much.

Back at the house I showed the letter to Jo. 'I know no more than you do,' she said when she had handed it back to me. 'It's something to do with his desk and what's in it, obviously. Let's go and have a look.'

The desk was a vast ornate piece of solid Victoriana, carved and knobbled on all exposed surfaces, with, facing its occupant, a curved bow containing cubbyholes, the ends of which joined a bank of small drawers on either side.

We went through the whole thing but our search revealed

remarkably little, for he must have had a cleaning out before he died. There were a couple of files relating to training matters for the one or two friends whose horses he still had, an entry ledger, a gallop book and nothing much else.

'What's this?' I said as I leafed through the gallop book and found at the end a list of figures under the heading *Video*.

'It's an index to his video tapes,' she said, looking over my shoulder. 'He took a tape of any of his own races that were on TV and most of the English and Irish ones too. He used to play them over to himself and work out imaginary handicaps. It was a sort of hobby. There they all are.' She pointed to an open cabinet in the corner.

'That's it, then,' I said, sitting back in the chair, closing the book and staring at the range of cubbyholes in front of me. 'Nothing. Where do we go from here? If there was anything there it's gone. Maybe they found it. Perhaps he changed his mind.'

'I don't believe it,' she said. 'He'd never have changed his mind. That wasn't him at all. If only he didn't always want to cloak things up—'

We both sat and glared at the inanimate desk, willing it to give up its secret if it had one. I let my gaze wander round the room, at the hunting prints on the walls, the regimental groups and the pictures of the Colonel's winners with himself in his young days up on some of them. It had been his sort of inviolable sanctuary when we were young, I remembered, and we had been forbidden to enter it save when requested—or ordered—to do so. It had no very happy memories for me, since my visits to it were mostly concerned with the matter of school reports or other sins I had committed, though Jo told me that recently she and the Colonel had used it as their living-room when they were alone and indeed there were signs of such use. The grog tray stood on a table in one corner and the television and video in another. I didn't want the damn desk anyway I told myself, looking at it again, and I knew he had only left it to me to call attention to whatever message he wanted to send from beyond the grave.

Jo meanwhile had continued to run her eyes over every bit of the ugly great thing. Suddenly she gave an exclamation and grabbed my arm. 'I think I've got it,' she said excitedly.

'Got what?' I said. 'It's been cleaned out. It's empty. That's all there is to it.'

'Look at the bow in front of you, at the cubbyholes.'

'All right, I'm looking.' Where the ends of the bow met the drawers to form a sort of platform the space between them was filled by two Corinthian pillars the tops of which were adorned by carved mahogany sunflowers.

'I remember now,' she said. 'Once when I was a kid I saw him opening it and he told me about it and how it worked. There's a secret drawer. Put your finger on the centre of that right-hand flower and push.'

I did as I was told and was rewarded by a faint click coming from behind the carving.

'Now turn it and pull,' she said.

Her memory had not played her false, for the carving turned stiffly beneath my hand. When I pulled it towards me the whole pillar and its surround came away to reveal a long, narrow box. Inside this box, standing upright, was a Luger automatic pistol with beside it two charged magazines. I lifted it out and felt for the action.

'Put that horrid thing down, Charles,' she said. 'You always were cack-handed with guns. Do you even know how it works?'

'I know enough to see if it's loaded,' I said, sliding back the action. 'There's nothing in the breech and no magazine in the butt either.'

'Even so, just don't point it at me. The Colonel always

said it was the unloaded ones that killed you. It'd be just like you to let it go off.'

I sighed and put the pistol down on the desk. I supposed I'd remain the fool of the family for the rest of my days. 'We've now got a gun,' I said, 'and much help that's going to be to us. Where do we go from here?'

'Hang on,' she said, putting her hand into the box. 'There's an envelope here too.' She lifted it out and looked at it. 'Addressed to you,' she said. 'Open it and see what's in it. It must be what he was hiding for us.'

Putting my thumb under the flap, I tore it open. Inside there was only a slip of paper. On it was written in the Colonel's handwriting, '*The gun might come in useful, you never know. I took it off a dead German. Third rack. Number ten.*' I read it out to her.

'More damn riddles,' I said. 'What the hell is he up to now?'

CHAPTER 5

'Well then, what about those brains of yours we used to hear so much of,' she said as we stared at the sheet of paper. 'Can't they produce an answer?'

'They're turning over,' I said. 'I'm surprised you can't hear the machinery working. And as a matter of fact I think they've just come up with something. Where's that gallop book?'

She leant forward, took it from the desk and handed it to me. Opening it, I leafed through the pages until I came to the one marked *Video*. 'There you are,' I said, pointing. 'He had them all listed in the same way under racks and numbers. He wrote the subject against the entry. What figures are on that paper?'

'Rack three, number ten,' she said, reading from it. 'What has he as the subject?'

'Leopardstown Chase,' I said. 'That doesn't sound very promising but let's have a look anyway.'

Together we crossed to the rack that held the tapes. I checked the numbers, took out the box and saw that the cassette was inside. When we had set it up in the video I think we both held our breaths as I pressed the play button.

At first it seemed just another tape of a race. The horses duly passed the post and afterwards we saw them crossing the parade ring towards the enclosures reserved for the placed horses. I scanned the faces around them but failed to recognize anyone.

'Any familiar faces? Anything there to ring a bell?' I asked her.

She shook her head. 'Only old Josh Duggan the trainer,' she said, 'and he had nothing to do with this, that I'll swear. He's about eighty and senile.'

'There was nothing in the running either,' I said. 'I'm blessed if I know what the Colonel was up to or what he meant—'

And then, suddenly, with a jerk, the whole scene changed. For a start we were back in black and white. First a country house came into view, a big Georgian affair with spreading wings. A group of men in military uniforms were lounging about the steps leading to the front door. The uniforms themselves were a variegated lot. Some of the loungers wore khaki service dress and dark trousers, others had dark tunics and khaki slacks or riding breeches and puttees. One thing they all had in common: every one of them save those that were bare-headed wore a rakish, dark-coloured glengarry.

'Who the hell are those?' I said.

'Auxiliaries,' she answered. 'The officer types of the Black and Tans in the Troubles. I often heard the Colonel talk of them and saw pictures he had of them. He was fascinated by that time, you know, and has a collection of books about it.'

'Where'd he get this tape, though?'

'He must have taped it from one of those histories of Ireland that were on the box a bit back while you were away. Look—'

As we watched a lorry bristling with armed men appeared in the picture. It drew up on the sweep in front of the house and its occupants began to jump down. They had been in action somewhere, for one of them had a bandage tied roughly round his head. The last to leave were two big, burly chaps; between them they had what was obviously a prisoner. Either he, too, was wounded or else he had been knocked about a bit, for his two escorts half carried, half dragged him towards the house. They went up the steps with him between them. When they reached the top he faced the camera for a brief moment and then the three of them disappeared inside.

At that moment there was an interruption. The Colonel's office was in the new wing between the library and the billiard room and it commanded a view of the back avenue leading to the stableyard. Looking out, Jo saw a car turning into it. She gave an exclamation. 'That's the Craddockscourt Range-Rover,' she said. 'Amory must be coming to visit us. I'll have to go and see what he wants. You'd better come along and be introduced.'

I pressed the stop button and followed her out.

The Range-Rover swept under the far archway and pulled up. The doors opened and three people spilled out. One was a tall, rather good-looking man who had been sitting in the front passenger seat; the driver was a young guy in a lumber jacket who walked like a horseman and moved as if he had springs in his heels. The third figure who clambered out of the back and followed them as they walked towards us I had no difficulty at all in recognizing. He was none other than my old pal whom I had last seen dancing about like a lunatic after I had clocked him behind the ear with a champagne cork—Francis Aloysius O'Shaughnessy.

I had no wish to encounter him again. Thinking I would employ my old trick of fading into the background, I moved slowly away. It didn't work. Those little pig's eyes of his missed nothing. 'Whoa there,' he shouted at me.

Pretending not to hear, I went on retreating.

'Hey, you! You there! Hold up!' he bellowed.

This time there was no mistaking it or pretending to. He meant me; I was collared. I turned slowly and stared at him. He was wearing a zipped-up lightweight anorak decorated with red and yellow stripes. I felt like asking him if he was advertising his racing colours. 'Are you meaning me?' I said.

'Who the hell do you think I mean?' he roared.

'I thought you must be addressing a horse,' I told him.

He gave me a baleful look as I approached. 'I've seen you before,' he said. 'I never forget a face—or a horse.'

'I don't recall it,' I said. 'And I could scarcely have forgotten you.' I looked pointedly at his jacket.

At this juncture Jo intervened to make the introductions. The tall, rather good-looking chap was Amory Brayne, millionaire, recently arrived and of whom I had heard, the young driver Jack Manley, rough-rider and general dogsbody, I gathered, while, as I knew, the third was Francis Aloysius O'Shaughnessy, bloodstock agent to the rich and great until, as someone had said, they found him out.

They asked if they could see the horses and, when Jo agreed, O'Shaughnessy and the young guy moved towards the boxes while Brayne remained talking to Jo. It didn't appear as if my presence was required so I gently faded away. Inside the house I remembered that Jo had said Mrs Connolly didn't come that day and that if I wanted my bed made I had better do it myself. I went up to the room, pulled the sheets and blankets into some sort of order and crossed to the window deep in thought. I remembered the thug's description of the geezer in the pub who had given him fifty nicker to rough me up. He had had a coat with 'checks as big as soup plates', which was just the sort of coat O'Shaughnessy would wear. I also remembered the reputation he had which had been described to me when I worked at the stud that if you crossed him you were likely to have unwelcome visitors. Well, I'd had one. Could it be that O'Shaughnessy was in some way connected with the Colonel's murder? It seemed fantastic on the face of it, for what possible reason could be behind it if he was, but those similarities, clues or whatever you liked to call them pointed that way. I wanted to dismiss the whole thing as a far-fetched coincidence but somehow I couldn't.

From my room I could see into the stableyard and, looking down, I watched O'Shaughnessy and Jack Manley going steadily along the row of boxes examining each inmate as they went. When they left the last box they came under the archway and up the path to the house. Jo and Brayne had moved away and were out of my sight.

After a bit I began to wonder just what O'Shaughnessy and his sidekick were doing in the house. There was no sign of the others, so I thought, rather against my will, that I had better go down and investigate. I found them in the Colonel's office.

O'Shaughnessy was sprawled in a chair by the hearth, in his hand a very brown glass of whisky which I assumed he had helped himself to from the grog tray. The sight of this gross bully occupying as of right and lording it in the chair which had always been the Colonel's particular preserve stirred in me all my resentment of him and what he stood for. Because this resentment had been triggered off by his usurpation of the Colonel's chair, it also reminded me that however much I might fight against them there were ties of birth and kinship which bound me to this family. And of this family only Jo was left. It wasn't until much later that I realized what this meant, too.

Jack Manley was standing by the desk and to my annoyance I saw that I had left the Colonel's message lying on it. 'Looking for something?' I said to him.

'Admiring it,' he said. 'It's a quaint old piece, isn't it?' He had a gin and tonic in his hand. 'Hope you don't mind,' he said. 'Jo told us to help ourselves.' He smiled as he said it. He had rather a charming smile. It was all innocent enough. I told myself I was a fool to think of any criminal connection there and went to fix myself a drink, but I wondered just the same if they had read the letter.

'That's a nice three-year-old,' Jack Manley said. 'In the third box down.'

'By Smash Hit out of Woebegone,' O'Shaughnessy's voice cut in. 'She bred three winners on the flat, two over hurdles and four chases. She's by Ten Per Cent—' He rattled off the back breeding for generations. 'I wasn't too keen on her hind leg,' he went on when he had paused for breath. Then he took a swig at his whisky, and glared at me again. 'I'll place you in a minute,' he said. 'What did you say your name was?'

'I didn't,' I said. 'But if it's anything to you it's Charles Hampton—at your service.'

He didn't quite know what to make of that and perhaps it was just as well that at that moment the door opened and Jo and Amory Brayne came in.

As soon as she entered I saw Jack Manley looking at her with adoring eyes. He fussed around her at the drink table, helping with the second drinks and making an excuse every now and then to touch her hand or her arm. I wondered vaguely what else he had touched and if there was anything between them. Anyway it was clear she had made a conquest. Nor did I find it surprising. She was, as I have said, a very attractive girl.

Brayne, unlike his henchman, was all charm and politeness. He crossed to me saying how glad he was to have met me. 'Jo told me you were the executor,' he said. 'I do hope for her sake you will find things not too bad financially. I had become friendly with them, you know, since I came here. Terrible thing about Colonel Manners. Is there any news of progress by the police?'

'None at all,' I said. 'It looks like another unsolved crime. They seem satisfied that it was subversives.'

'You know, I'm sure, that if there's anything I can do—'

'Of course,' I said. 'And I know Jo is very grateful.'

They left shortly after that and when they had gone Jo turned to me, perhaps turned on me would be a better description. 'You were a great help, I must say,' she said. 'Why were you so rude to Francis Aloysius?'

'That bastard,' I said, and I told her of our encounter and of the champagne cork. I did not tell her of my suspicions. They were too vague as yet, nor did I tell her of the attack on me. There was no point in frightening her and adding to her worries. When I had finished she laughed.

'The Colonel always said he was shit,' she said. 'But he used to add that he was a damn good bloodstock agent—when he wanted to be and was on your side.'

'And Jack Manley,' I said. 'I saw him making sheeps' eyes, whatever they may be, at you. You've got him hooked and dangling.'

'Jack? Don't be a damn fool. He came to them with the place. He had joined Dick as his assistant and was trying to pull the stud round but Dick wouldn't listen to anyone, as you'll recall if you remember him. Then the crash came and Dick went bust. When Amory bought the place he took Jack on. I think the Colonel advised him to. He said Jack had a damn good eye.'

'And not for horses only, it seems,' I said.

'Shut up. If I was near enough to you I'd kick you.'

'And O'Shaughnessy,' I said. 'How does he come into it?'

'He was there already. He looked after Amory's bloodstock interests in the States, so it was natural for Amory to bring him along when he bought Craddockscourt. He's the adviser and manager and boss, if you ask me. I don't think Amory knows much about bloodstock or racing. He hasn't been in it very long. He's burying tax money, I suppose, like a lot of these chaps, and he's been lucky. They won the Guineas this year with Midsummer Day and they say he'll win the Irish Derby, so Francis Aloysius hasn't done him badly.'

'I see,' I said. 'Well, good luck to them. In the meantime we'd better get back to business and have another look at the tape to see if it tells us anything.' I picked up the remote control.

'Play it again, Sam,' she said, looking at me mischievously.

'She never said that, as I told you before,' I said as I pressed the button.

The video clicked, and whirled. A picture of Francis Aloysius, beaming as he stood beside Brayne in the winners' enclosure after the Two Thousand Guineas, appeared on the screen. 'Hold it,' I said, realization coming to me as I snapped down the stop button. 'That's not where we ran it to when we went out. Someone else has been playing the tape.'

We stared at each other in silence.

'Guess who?' I said.

'Francis Aloysius—' she breathed.

'None other, I'll lay the odds. Either he read the Colonel's message I left lying on the desk or else played it on spec. It must have given him something to think about to see his ugly mug come to look at him.'

'But what does it all mean?'

'Search me. Did the Colonel often splice up tapes like this?'

'Oh yes. It was a sort of hobby with him. He said you could do anything with tapes if you knew how to use them.'

'He's certainly done something with this one. I only wish we knew what it was. Wait a bit. I may have got it.' I rewound the tape and when it came to the Auxiliaries' captive facing the camera I stopped it. 'Have a good look at him,' I said. After a moment I ran the tape on again and when it came to O'Shaughnessy and the Guineas winner I stopped it there. 'See what I mean?' I said.

'The resemblance,' she said. 'Francis Aloysius is a dead ringer for that prisoner—'

'Exactly.'

'They can't be the same man—'

'No. The age difference is too great. But there's a relationship somewhere. My guess is that he's a son. Let's see if there's anything more. The Colonel's been laying some sort of trail.' I ran the tape on. First there appeared a frame of the house where the Auxiliaries had brought their captive and next a posed studio portrait of a man dressed for the occasion wearing a dark suit and a wing collar. Even though it was blurred by poor reproduction, his identity was unmistakable. It was the captive. Also unmistakable was the resemblance to O'Shaughnessy. The tape ran on and no further pictures appeared.

I stared at the blank screen. 'I wonder,' I said. 'You said he had a collection of books about The Troubles. Could they tell us something?'

'They're all there.' She pointed to a bookcase by the fireplace.

'That clip was taken from one of the documentaries and they got it from a book. Wait a bit. Maybe it tells us where to look.' I ran the tape again and at the very top, over the picture, we could make out the words, *Munster's Freedom Fighters*. 'That's it,' I said.

'There should be a book with that title. Let's see if we can find it.'

Mostly the bookcase was crammed with volumes of *The Racing Calendar* and *The Bloodstock Breeders Review* together with a few books of racing reminiscences by those whom the Colonel considered to be 'proper chaps', of whom there weren't all that many. The ones that concerned themselves with the struggle of seventy-odd years before were on a lower shelf. 'There they are,' she said. 'He got them when they came out ages ago, before I was born.' She pulled out several fat paperbacks, slightly soiled and spotted with age. 'It'll be one of these. Here it is—*Munster's Freedom Fighters*.'

She handed me the book. Its cover bore a picture of a man with a bandolier and a World War I Lee Enfield at the ready against a background of a Rolls-Royce armoured car and a collection of troops in the motley of uniforms I had seen on the tape.

'With any luck this will tell us who the captive was,' I said.

As it happened, we had not far to look. From one of the early pages the portrait stared back at us. *Commandant Seumas O'Shaughnessy* was the caption and underneath was a potted biography:

> Seumas O'Shaughnessy's father was a member of a Ballinamorra, County Kilderry family evicted and forced to emigrate to America on one of the landlord's infamous coffin ships. Settling in Minnesota, he married and raised a large family of which Seumas was the eldest son. Nurtured in a staunch Republican tradition, young Seumas returned to Ireland about 1910 and joined the Volunteers, in preparation for taking up arms against the occupying

forces. He fought in the GPO in 1916, was taken prisoner and condemned to death but was subsequently reprieved. In the Black and Tan War he commanded the Kilderry Flying Column with conspicuous success, was captured by the Auxiliaries after the fight at Barra Bridge. While a prisoner in their hands he escaped. In the Civil War he joined the anti-Treaty forces and on disbandment returned to Ballinamorra.

'The ending is pretty cryptic,' I said. 'It doesn't tell us what happened to him afterwards and whether he married or whatever. If Francis Aloysius is a son or close relative he doesn't want to disclose it for reasons of his own, and that means—'

'That he's connected with the subversives,' she said. 'So it looks as if the official version is right after all.'

'Up to a point, Lord Copper.'

'What do you mean by that? Stop being clever-clever, Charles.'

'I wonder if it does mean just that. There are a whole lot of unanswered questions. Why did the Colonel go to all this trouble? He'd found out something yet he wasn't quite sure . . . Anyway, now the first thing for us to do is to try to find out where O'Shaughnessy fits in with the rest of the picture and just who he was or rather is. Does the *Directory of The Turf* help—he's bound to be in it?'

I took the book from the shelf and turned to the Owners section. The entry O'Shaughnessy had made for himself was brief. He gave an address at Lexington, Kentucky, and another in London. His best horse owned was Malvolio, winner of the Stewards' Cup a few years back and his date of birth was 30th October 1930. His racing colours were orange and black. That was all, just enough to tell an inquirer something, to indicate that he had nothing to hide and yet not to give anything conclusive away, or that's how it looked to my suspicious mind. 'Not much help,' I said, 'but at least we know when he was born—if he's telling the truth.'

At that moment the telephone rang. Jo picked up the receiver and when she had listened for a moment handed it to me. 'It's for you.'

It was Denzil Colton. 'Thought you might like to know,' he said. 'I asked my father about your guardian, Colonel Manners, and the SOE. He's pretty ga-ga, poor old Pa, but he did remember something. Your guardian's lot walked into some sort of trap and only one or two got out. Colonel Manners was one of them.'

'Did he tell you anything more?'

'No. Except he thought they were based somewhere in the Pyrenees. The survivors escaped through Spain. Have you found anything your end?'

'Nothing much,' I said. 'If your pa remembers anything more, let me know, will you?'

'Sure thing. He said he'd keep trying. There are one or two contacts he still has. It's given him an interest and it might do him a bit of good. Apart from that he's keeping going on vintage port and it's a question which of them lasts the longer—him or the cellar.'

'What's all that?' she asked me as I replaced the receiver.

'My old number one in the Gulf. His father was in the SOE. I asked him to try to find out something about the Colonel's service with them.'

'And has he?'

'A bit. His pa remembers something, even though apparently he's relying on vintage port to keep the blood flowing through his veins. The Colonel's lot were ambushed or something and he was lucky to get out.'

'But can that have anything to do with his killing? It does look like subversives now.'

'But I still wonder. We're groping in the dark.'

'Why, oh why, didn't the Colonel leave a letter or something for us telling it all in the clear?'

'My guess is he wasn't sure himself just what he'd stumbled into and was killed because someone else was frightened he knew too much. Anyway, one thing is for sure and that is O'Shaughnessy is mixed up in it somewhere. Whether Brayne is too is another matter. That picture of the two of them together must have meant something.'

'I can't believe Amory is. The Colonel liked him. He said he couldn't understand why he seemed to rely so much on Francis Aloysius. He had him round the place like a sort of grand vizier, he said.'

'Maybe he did understand in the end. Maybe that's what he found out. At all events, the first thing for us to do is to discover just who O'Shaughnessy is. The place for that is that village Ballinamorra, I should think. I'll go there tomorrow and make inquiries. There'll be some sort of register somewhere, I suppose. The question is, where do I start.'

'That's no problem,' Jo said. 'Try the parish priest.'

CHAPTER 6

Ballinamorra, like many another remote Irish village, consisted of one long, straggling street. It was bisected by a crossroad which at its junction formed an open space. In the centre of this was a statue of a man striding forward with a revolver in his outstretched hand. I stopped the car and got out to have a look at it. It was lifesize and striking. The figure was hatless, the wind was in his hair and he looked over the houses to the blue hazy mountains beyond them. On the plinth beneath his feet was the inscription: *Commandant Seumas O'Shaughnessy. Fighter For Freedom.* Below this were words in Irish which I could not translate. On a closer look the statue appeared uncared-for. It was spattered with pigeon droppings and some of the lettering on the plinth had chipped and fallen away. Seumas O'Shaughnessy had been a hero in his time but that was seventy years ago and even Irish memories fade with the years. Thoughtfully I returned to the car.

At the far end of the street I could see the Catholic church set on a little hill and dominating the whole place. Beside it was the priest's house, a square block painted blue with a glass porch in front of it and a short cement driveway leading up to it. I stopped the car by the gate and walked up the drive.

The door was opened by a motherly body in a print frock whom I took to be the housekeeper. Father Milligan was in, she said, and brought me down a passage to a door at the farther end. Knocking on it, she motioned me to wait and went in. After a moment or two she came back. 'He'll see you now,' she said.

It was a spare, austere and rather comfortless room. There was a holy picture on one wall, on the mantelpiece a statue of Child Jesus of Prague, a wooden crucifix and a picture of the Pope. The furniture consisted of an oak desk across one corner, a glass-fronted Victorian bookcase and two worn leather chairs. In one of these the priest was sitting reading from a breviary. As I entered he carefully placed a bookmark in the breviary, closed it and stood up. He was a grey-haired, tall, ascetic, and scholarly-looking man.

With the story I had prepared ready on my lips I explained my errand to him. A friend, I said, had asked me to try and trace his relations. He was looking for a record of birth. He could not come himself for business reasons but learning that I would be in Ireland had asked me if I was in the vicinity would I call in to Ballinamorra.

Of course, he said. He would be glad to do what he

could to help. He had many such inquiries especially from Americans. He had had one such only yesterday. The books of record were in the vestry and he would take me there.

The priest's house adjoined the church; together we entered by a side door and crossed the nave, where he genuflected in front of the altar and I awkwardly followed suit. Observing me, he smiled briefly. 'You are one of our separated brethren, I perceive,' he said. 'But all are welcome here. In my father's house there are many mansions.' He opened the vestry door.

The Registers, leather-bound and some of them worn and battered with age, were stacked on a table against a wall. He asked me if I had a date to begin my search. I told him October 1930 and after moving the volumes about he selected one and began to leaf through the pages. All of a sudden he stopped, frowning. 'That's strange,' he said. 'Very strange indeed.'

'What is it?' I said, peering over his shoulder.

He turned to look at me and our eyes met. 'The page you are seeking has been torn out,' he said.

'But,' I said, 'how could that happen? Who could have done it and why?' Though even as I spoke I had a pretty good idea of the answer to both questions.

He had turned back again to examine the opened ledger. 'It's very disturbing,' he said. 'You know, in those days not long after the Civil War when things had scarcely returned to normal, births and deaths from these remote districts were frequently not registered in the central registry at all. These baptismal records are the only source of information and verification and now this whole page has gone—'

'Perhaps I'm being impertinent,' I said, 'but could it have been the visitor you had yesterday?'

He frowned once more. 'Now you mention it,' he said, 'it may well have been. I was called away to the telephone and left him here. When I returned he had gone. At the time I thought it odd that he should have left without a word of thanks or to say whether or not his search had been successful.'

'May I ask what he was like?' I said.

'Indeed you may. He was a large man, rather brusque and demanding in manner. He gave me no details. He said, now I recall, that he knew his way about such things and would make his own search. One other thing: he was wearing a coat or anorak of striking design. A coat of many colours I mentally thought of it.'

'I see,' I said.

'Perhaps you know him.' He gave me a piercing look.

'I think I may do,' I said.

'Now it is I who am being impertinent. I always hesitate to ask details of these inquiries since they involve family matters which are usually confidential and sometimes distasteful. But in this instance, in view of what has happened, I think I may. Are you at liberty to tell me what family of the parish it is whose records you are pursuing?'

I hesitated. Then I said, 'My friend believed himself related to the O'Shaughnessy family. Seumas O'Shaughnessy was, I gather, a leader in the Troubles and a local hero. As a matter of fact, I saw a statue of him as I was driving through the village. My friend was anxious to establish the connection. Now that the page has gone perhaps you can tell me something about the family.'

He looked at me shrewdly as if he knew very well he was not being told the whole truth. Then he closed the ledger. 'Since your journey has been fruitless owing to my carelessness in leaving my visitor alone, I shall do what I can to help. Come along,' he said.

He led the way back to the house. In the hallway we met the housekeeper. 'Ah, Agnes, the whisky,' he said as he opened the door to his study and motioned me to one of the armchairs.

The whisky came in a cut-glass decanter accompanied by two antique Waterford glass goblets into which he poured generous measures. Settling himself in his chair, he sipped his drink. 'It all happened, of course, long ago, long before I came here,' he began. 'But I have always, wherever I have been, taken an interest in local history and Seumas O'Shaughnessy was at one time, as you say, something of a hero to the village. At first it appeared to be a romantic story, though sadly it did not turn out that way.'

He paused. He was, it seemed to me, quite glad of an audience and I remembered hearing somewhere that parish priests of the older austere type, unlike the trendy, back-slappers now in vogue, led lonely lives. But he was going on: 'As I've said,' he continued, 'Seumas O'Shaughnessy was a hero of his time. I use the past tense advisedly since memories are growing dim and the young, and perhaps it is a good sign, are no longer interested in those terrible years. You are young yourself Mr—I don't think you ever told me your name.'

'Hampton,' I said, and as soon as I had I regretted I had not invented another one on the spur of the moment in case anyone came inquiring, though even as that thought crossed my mind I told myself I didn't want to deceive this kindly old man more than I was already doing.

'Well, Mr Hampton, from your voice I assume you to be an Englishman so perhaps you know little of our history and our struggle for independence.'

'I do know something,' I said.

'First we fought for our freedom, the Black and Tan War as it is sometimes called. Then, when we had won it, we had a dreadful civil war between those who favoured the treaty with England and those who opposed it on the grounds that it did not grant us full Republican status. Seumas O'Shaughnessy elected to go with those who opposed the Treaty. In one of the last engagements before their final defeat by the Free State Forces he was very severely wounded.' He took a sip from his drink while I waited expectantly.

'At that time,' he went on, 'the leaders of the anti-Treaty forces were being ruthlessly hunted down and in some cases shot out of hand. Somehow Seumas made his way back here, to his roots. He was hidden by a family whom he had known in the early days of the movement. They concealed his presence and the daughter of the house devotedly nursed him back to strength. It was a long illness and convalescence and by the time he had recovered much of the hue and cry had died down. He married the girl. The family had a small grocery and publican's business in the village. They had no son. He and his wife took it over.'

'And then?' I said, for I knew this was not the end of the story.

'The marriage and the business failed. He was still troubled by his wounds and in constant pain. In addition he was embittered by the way things had turned out politically, or so I was told. The Treaty forces were in power then under Cosgrave and survivors of their enemies could expect no help from them. He became his own best customer behind the bar. She turned into a termagant. The erection of the statue financed by sympathizers in America only served to remind him of his days of glory. He hated it, I believe. The upshot of it all was that he took himself, his wife and his family off to America and cut off all his ties with the homeland.'

'You mention family. What did it consist of?'

'A boy and a girl, I believe.'

'Did they or any of them ever return?'

'Not to my knowledge. Efforts were made to trace them but without success. It was the time of the great Depression. There was a suggestion that both the parents had died and that the children had been farmed out to foster parents who were also refugees, one would call them now. Be that as it may, so far as Ballinamorra was concerned they simply disappeared into the vastness of America and with the passing of the years they have become forgotten. Even the statue, as you may have noticed, is falling into disrepair. The young have short memories. No one appears to have given them a thought. That is to say until now—' He looked at me speculatively and I guessed what he had in mind.

'No, Father,' I said. 'I am not a blood relation or any relation at all for that matter, but I'll tell my friend what I've learnt and I'm grateful to you for giving me your time—'

He smiled slightly. 'My time is of little account,' he said, 'it's been a pleasure talking to you.'

I refused a second drink and took my leave.

My way back to Pollardstown brought me past Bilby Barrows's demesne. I had forgotten its name but I recognized the entrance gates when I saw them. I remembered then Jo telling me that he had been unable to attend the funeral and when making his excuses for his absence had told her that he had had a puzzling letter from the Colonel a little while before.

On impulse I turned through the gates. The roof of the lodge had fallen in, I saw, and the avenue up which I bumped was pitted and rutted. When I reached what had been the gravel sweep in front of the house I found its windows and doorway boarded up and its façade, empty of life, stared blankly at me.

I was staring back at it wondering what had become of its owner and remembering childhood parties in its long airy rooms when a man came round a corner of the house and approached the car. He was wearing an open-necked shirt, an old tweed coat and a pair of baggy corduroy trousers which had probably first seen service in the Western Desert. At his heels were two brown and white terriers. 'And what do you want?' he barked at me in military tones, and then, looking at me more closely through the open window of the car: 'I know you. You're young Hampton from Pollardstown. I remember you from the Pony Club. Learnt to ride yet?'

'Not so you'd notice,' I said.

'Surprised to see this, are you?' He waved a hand towards the empty house. 'Couldn't pay for a new roof and got tired of moving from room to room as the water came in. Couldn't flog it to any of these new people, Yanks and Arabs. Not enough land, they said. Only things they want are stud farms and leisure centres, whatever they are. Come about poor old Tom Manners's death, I expect, have you?'

'As a matter of fact I have,' I said. 'I believe he wrote you a letter—'

'He did and a damned odd one I must say. Come along, then.'

Leaving the car, we followed a path through the trees which were beginning to press all around the derelict house. After a little the path broadened into a clearing, in the centre of which was a small white-painted house with a tiled roof and a bow window. 'Gamekeeper's cottage,' he said, 'and my new abode. Come in.'

The living-room was built round the window. In its curve were a hunting table and Hepplewhite chairs obviously salvaged from the big house. Chintz-covered armchairs and a sofa stood in front of the fireplace. On the walls were Snaffles prints and regimental groups. A gun-rack stood beside a serving hatch in one corner. He banged on this and it flew open at once. A red face with a bristling moustache peered out. 'Tea, is it,' came from its lips. 'And someone wid ye. That's a change.' The hatch slammed shut.

'My ex-soldier servant,' Barrows explained. 'Not noted

for his civility. I usually have tea at this time. I hope you'll join me.'

I suddenly remembered that what with one thing or another I hadn't had any lunch and told him I'd be glad to.

Tea was served by the soldier servant now wearing a khaki alpaca jacket with regimental buttons. There was a silver tea service, a fruit cake and sardine sandwiches. I felt like asking Barrows if he still dressed for dinner.

'It's Indian, none of your Chinese nonsense here,' the servitor barked at me as he withdrew.

Barrows took not the least notice but began to munch the sandwiches, absent-mindedly passing me the plate and feeding others to the two dogs who eyed him expectantly. 'Now then,' he said. 'How can I help you? I may be of precious little use.'

'About that letter,' I said.

'Damned odd, as I've said, and pretty short. He said he wanted to see me. Something had come up, something out of the past and it was embarrassing to say the least. Embarrassing, that was the word he used. Very odd, I thought. Next thing I knew he was dead—killed.'

'Jo thinks it might have had something to do with his time in the SOE from what little he said to her. I have a friend whose father was in it. He said they walked into some sort of trap. Do you know anything about it?'

'Precious little, I'm afraid. He seldom spoke of it. But odd things, and that's putting it mildly, did happen in that organization. Dark deeds were done. In my opinion SOE was one of Churchill's blunders.'

'Can you tell me more?'

'You're too young to know about those days of the war. If you think of Churchill at all I suppose you know of him as a great man, the saviour of the country who beat the Nazis. He was all of that, but he was also an adventurer and he loved private armies. He'd been a sort of private army of his own in his youth. That was why he dreamed up SOE—set Europe ablaze sort of tosh. There was a perfectly good organization ready for doing just that, and as a result of his setting up another all sort of odd bods crept out of the woodwork into SOE.'

'How did the Colonel get into it?'

'He was always a bit of an irregular soldier himself, you know. He was with Jock Columns early in the war. You won't know what they were and it would take too long to tell you. In the end he had an almighty row with one of Monty's pals just before Alamein and was sent home. He was pretty bitter about it and when he got back somehow he wangled himself into SOE and was dropped into France. He was there for some time with the Resistance, but he didn't talk about it. He could be very secretive, you know.'

'Is it possible that it had anything to do with his killing? He does seem to have been harking back, from what Jo said, and then there is that strange letter to you.'

'It's possible, I suppose, but it's unlikely, isn't it? It's all so long ago.'

'Do you think then that it was subversives who killed him?'

'I don't know. If they didn't, who did? I can't think of anyone else. Can you?'

'Yes,' I said. 'I can.' I told him something of the trail of clues the Colonel had left and what I had discovered about O'Shaughnessy.

'O'Shaughnessy—eh?' he said. 'That chap. It wouldn't surprise me much to find that he's mixed up in it somewhere. You know the bad men in the bloodstock business, they're a mixture of a tout and a tart with the worst elements of both and a bit of the ham actor thrown in, and he's one of them. But he knows his job, make no mistake about that. But if he is in it, why is he?'

'That's just what's puzzling us,' I said. 'The Colonel left

these clues but they're maddening. They go just so far and no farther.'

'I suppose,' he said slowly, as if thinking it over in his mind, 'that O'Shaughnessy from what you have found out could have subversive connections he's trying to hide and that Tom discovered them.'

'But there are all sorts of unanswered questions,' I said. 'Why did he keep telling Jo it was something from his past that was bothering him and hinting that it had to do with his time in SOE? Why did he tell you that it was embarrassing and why did he leave that strange letter to me? I can't help thinking there's more behind it. And Brayne—he kept that clip on the tape of Brayne and O'Shaughnessy together, if that means anything. Where does he come into it, or does he?'

'I shouldn't think so. O'Shaughnessy picked him up in the States when Brayne was getting himself into racing. Like a lot of these chaps who have made a pile, Brayne, I suppose, wanted to cash in on the tax advantages of bloodstock owning and get a bit of prestige at the same time. But he isn't a pushy sort of chap like a lot of our homebreds, I regret to say. He's retiring, if anything. He's well liked. There's talk of putting him up for the Turf Club. He'd be better than some, I must say.'

'He's Mr Clean, in fact,' I said.

'That's about it. It fits him. And remember they've been very successful, the Guineas this year and that, I'm told, is a bloody good colt.'

'Is that the colt Jo told me they fancied for the Irish Derby?'

'That's right. Midsummer Day. They didn't run him at Epsom. They're keeping him for the Curragh, I believe. They say the track will suit him better.'

'When you say "they" I suppose you mean O'Shaughnessy. He's the racing manager, isn't he?'

'So far as I know he's everything where the horses are concerned. He buys 'em, he breeds 'em and he runs 'em. The only thing he doesn't do is train 'em, though I expect he has a hand in that too.'

'I still can't understand how Brayne, if he's all you say he is, allows himself to be run by a guy like O'Shaughnessy.'

He looked at me and smiled. 'You're young,' he said. 'And the young are intolerant. You and I don't like loud mouths but those are the fellers who are big in racing now—it's a business and the sport went out of it long ago. It's a blowhard's world, but don't let me go on about this, and I'm bound to say I've heard it said of O'Shaughnessy that he gives good service and doesn't sell his employers down the river like some of them do. And a chap like Brayne attracts hangers-on. O'Shaughnessy keeps them at bay—or kicks them out.'

'Because he wants it all himself,' I said.

He laughed aloud at that. 'I was just putting the other side of the coin,' he said. 'When I was your age I'd have felt the same about him. Age is a great mellower.'

'It didn't mellow the Colonel much,' I said.

'Don't be so sure. Forty years ago he wouldn't have hesitated, wouldn't have asked for help. He'd have gone straight for the jugular.'

'If he knew whose it was and where it was,' I said.

Silence fell between us then for a minute or two while the terriers looked up at him as if expecting more sandwiches to come. He was frowning; he picked up a pipe from a side table, fiddled with it and put it down. I waited, rather wondering what was coming next. Then he said, 'Now I recall it, he did say to me once, "Nice chap, Brayne. Strange thing is he reminds me of someone, can't think who." I only remembered this as we've been talking about him. Don't know if it means anything.'

*

When I got back to Pollardstown I found Jo sitting watching the news on television, or rather staring at the screen for she was clearly paying little attention to it. The fingers of one hand were drumming nervously on the arm of her chair and those of the other were plucking at her eyebrows in a manner I remembered from childhood when she was waiting to go into the show-jumping arena or start on a cross-country.

'What's up, Jo?' I said. 'Something is. You're giving those eyebrows a hard time.' That was what Mike used to say when he teased her and unconsciously I fell back into the idiom of the old days.

She looked at me blankly for a moment and then said, 'I went to the bank today.'

'Oh, and what had they to say?'

'They're not going to cash any more cheques.' She got up and began to pace round the room. 'What am I to do, Charles?' she said. 'There's the wages—Cassidy, Paddy the yard boy and Mrs Connolly. We're in hock so deep they won't ante up another penny. Bloody banks. The manager wasn't a bit nice about it. In fact he was damned rude. He's been warning the Colonel for years, he said, and now even if he wanted to, which he doesn't, it seems he can't give us any more credit, his directors won't let him.'

'Sit down,' I said. 'Take it easy and tell all.'

She went back to her chair while I poured her a drink. In the bank, she said, the cashier had hummed and hawed when she presented her cheque to discharge the weekly wages. It was drawn on the joint account she shared with the Colonel. The cashier had gone off with it and a minute or two later she had been summoned into the inner sanctum—'the bloody sweat-box', she called it—by the manager. He had, it seemed, given her such a going-over as almost to reduce her to tears.

'No small feat,' I said, hearing this.

The drink and the fact of sharing her woes had perked her up a bit. 'If I could find anything handy I'd throw it at you,' she said.

'In your present state you'd probably miss,' I told her. 'Try stamping your foot like Scarlett O'Hara. What happened next and did he offer you a handkerchief?'

'Not even a tissue. He knew he had me on the ropes and he was keeping me there. We'll have to sell, he said. And if we don't do it ourselves the bank will do it for us. And pretty quick too and what about it?'

'They used to say in the stud where I worked for a bit,' I said, 'that bank managers were splendid guys when they had your money and the biggest bastards of all when you had theirs and they wanted it back. And studs know more than a thing or two about banks one way or another. It seems they were right.'

'Anyway,' she went on, 'outside on the steps I ran into Amory. He saw I was upset and he took me off and gave me coffee. I was shaking by this time—'

'With rage, I imagine,' I said.

'Shut up. You're as bad as the bloody manager. Amory was a sight more sympathetic, let me tell you. He guessed something was wrong and he asked me about it. The long and the short of it was I blurted out the whole thing to him. You may be mad at me, Charles, for doing it and I don't care a tinker's curse if you are, for what happened was he said he might be interested in the place if we were putting it on the market. It could be the answer to everything.'

'It just might,' I said. 'But seriously, Jo, how do you feel about it? And what will you do?'

'You know how I'll hate leaving here. I love every stick and stone of the old place but somehow I've seen this coming and I've been, unconsciously, I think, toughening myself to take it. I think I've known for some time in my heart of hearts that if anything happened to the Colonel I couldn't carry on. As for what I'll do—something with horses, I suppose. They say once you can handle horses they never let you down.'

'Except on the race track when the buggers always do,' I said.

'Yes, well, I'm not exactly going to be an owner any more. Do you think Amory would help? Perhaps he'd let me stay on here for a bit while I straightened myself out. He did hint at something . . .'

A sprat to catch a mackerel, I thought to myself and then told myself I was being unfair. After all, he was Mr Clean, wasn't he? 'Did he mention a price?' I said.

'No. He said we'd want to get professional advice. He knew Davey acted for us and suggested we consult him. He was anxious to know pretty quickly as there was another property he'd been offered. He suggested we came to lunch tomorrow and talked the thing over. He was awfully *nice* about it, Charles.'

I felt the first faint stirrings of what long afterwards I came to realize was jealousy. 'Nice, was he?' I said. 'Too damn nice if you ask me. It's all very convenient, isn't it? By the way, has he a wife?'

'He had one but she's been gone for years. Camilla Harbury stands in. She's been with him for ages. You'll meet her tomorrow if she's there.'

'If we go. What about this professional advice? It's all a bit rushed, isn't it? When do we see the solicitor?'

'Tonight. I've asked him to supper.'

CHAPTER 7

Craddockscourt Castle was a ghastly house. That was what I thought seeing it for the first time since my boyhood as we came along the impeccably tarmaced drive to where its fake battlements, crockets and finials loomed through the mist, for it was raining, the soft Irish summer rain which didn't help to lessen its Gothic gloom.

Although as a boy I had hunted past it on a pony I had never before been inside it. Dick Willoughby did not concern himself with the young, being too busy entertaining his racing friends and acquaintances from the wilder shores of the Turf and trying to flog them shares in the third-rate stallions which others of his ilk had persuaded him to buy and which had contributed largely to the crash when it came. Not for nothing had he been known as Mr Scatter-cash.

There were three of us in the Porsche when I pulled it up under the massive and hideous porte-cochère, myself, Jo, and, cramped in the back, which he had insisted on occupying—'I'm only the hired help'— Paul Davey, the solicitor.

He had duly come to supper the night before, arriving looking tired, drawn and grey in the face. 'I've had a ghastly day,' he announced as he dropped into an armchair. 'Yes, please, Jo, I do want a whisky, a large one, perhaps I should say a very large one. I had a district court this morning,' he went on, as Jo handed him a glass tall and brown and brimming. 'It was before a strange district justice who because I speak an approximation of the Queen's English seems to have thought I was trying to put over on him the attitudes of the old Ascendancy or that I was a West Briton. I never understood what that term means but it's a current term of abuse, or some such rot. He kicked out every application I made, convicted one client of dangerous driving when there wasn't a shred of evidence to sustain the charge, and sent two others to gaol. In the afternoon I had a sale which erupted into a row over two rights of way no one had disclosed, and when I got back to the office I found that a caveat had been entered to a will I drew ten years ago and can't remember the first thing about. There must be an easier way of earning a living, if it is one, than this.'

'Oh Lord,' Jo said. 'I am sorry for dragging you over, Paul, but it did seem urgent and important.'

His whisky had disappeared in the space of that speech and she poured him another. Then she told him of her encounter with the bank manager and Amory Brayne's tentative offer.

He listened attentively and the end of her story came as he finished the second drink. Colour had come back to his cheeks and his eyes were brighter. He refused a third. 'Whisky is the best reviver of all,' he said. 'What would us poor lackeys do without it? The trouble is the temptation to do too much with it.'

'It looks as if it may be the last you'll get in this house, at least for a bit,' Jo said. 'What are we poor clients to do without money? That bloody bank manager—'

Davey's lips twitched into a brief smile. 'Don't be too hard on him,' he said. 'I rang him as soon as I heard from you. He'd just received a letter from his directors giving him all sorts of merry hell for allowing your father to go over the permitted limit of his account. Apparently the final straw was that he gave him additional credit to buy a share in the last of Dick Willoughby's bad stallions.'

'I always thought the Colonel said Dick Willoughby was a fool,' I said.

'So he did,' Jo put in, 'but I remember it all now. Hunter's Moon, it looked all right on paper, he'd won the Eclipse and the Colonel said it was worth a gamble. I didn't realize then it was a last gamble. Anyway, he turned out useless. I don't know where or how Dick got him.'

'Through O'Shaughnessy, I believe,' Davey said. 'He was useless, as you say. I acted for another shareholder. He was sold abroad at a loss and the shareholders lost their money.'

'Hunter's Moon,' I said. 'But hold on. He's the sire, isn't he, of Midsummer Day, that Classic colt of theirs. He's far from worthless now. How come he was sold for buttons?'

'It's a sad story,' Jo said. 'But I suppose you could say it has happened before. I'll tell it to you. Hunter's Moon was useless all right. He was sold to Japan, for buttons like you said, and the shareholders lost their money. Then Francis Aloysius got into the act. Hunter's Moon sired one or two minor winners in Japan and Francis Aloysius bought him back cheaply, saying he thought he'd nick with a couple of mares he'd bought Amory. He also said he'd advised Dick against selling him and Dick was the major shareholder and wouldn't take his advice. At least that's the story he told the Colonel when he went for him in no uncertain fashion about the whole deal.'

'And now he's got a Classic winner and the favourite for the Irish Derby,' I said.

'And Dick, in the end, lost Craddockscourt,' Jo said. 'Though I suppose he got something out of the wreck and it doesn't seem as if we have. I can't even cash a cheque.'

'I think I can probably fix that,' Davey said. 'But things are pretty bad, I'm afraid.'

'Just how bad,' I said. 'We might as well know the worst.'

He reached for his briefcase, opened it and took out a sheet of paper. 'I've prepared a brief run-down,' he said, 'And here's how it stands as I see it.'

We both waited while he put on his reading half-glasses and adjusted them. I stole a look at Jo. She had gone slightly pale and her fingers were clenched round her glass. I knew then that this was hitting her hard, whatever brave words she had said about being subconsciously prepared for it, and even though I was aware, none better, of the streak of toughness which ran through the family.

She'd had a rough day, she hadn't been brought up to dealing with bank managers at their worst; by and large so far she had only had to ask for what she wanted to be given it and the money was found somewhere. And now, I reckoned, she was on the point of being told that she was about to lose everything—her house, her horses and her way of life.

Davey's quiet voice was going on. 'The bank hold the deeds of Pollardstown,' he said. 'And they have a charge on it. As I mentioned, Colonel Manners's drawings far exceed his agreed and permitted limit. The bank are threatening to call in their charge.'

'Is that all?' I said. 'I think we know that already from Jo's encounter with the manager this morning.'

'No, it's not quite all. In addition to his bank borrowings Colonel Manners took a large loan from the Agricultural Credit Corporation at the time that they were handing out money as if there was no tomorrow.'

'I didn't know that,' Jo said. 'What was that for?'

'He told them it was to buy stock and machinery so as to make the place profitable on modern lines of farming. He used it to buy bloodstock, stores mostly, chasing stores and that's a risky business. Horses are dangerous stock—'

'Don't we know it,' Jo said. 'Don't *preach*, Paul. He lost one, others went wrong. That three-year-old by Smash Hit is about the only one likely to make anything.'

'Well then, what about the Agricultural Credit Corporation, whatever it is,' I said. 'Are they doing anything about the loan?'

'They're threatening to sue. The repayments are way in arrear and interest has piled up.'

'Is there any more bad news?' Jo said bitterly.

'There is more. I'm sorry to be the one to spell it out but you did ask and it's better that you know now and know it all. There are trade creditors, quite a few of them, and they are pressing. His social security returns for Cassidy and the yard boy are in arrear and in a mess. He hasn't properly accounted for PAYE and PRSI for months if not years and they are threatening to crack down, too.'

'How soon will that be?' I asked. It seemed, as well as the Colonel's personal problems and the manner of his death, I had landed myself into a nice mess as his executor.

'So now we know.' Jo's voice for once had a shake in it. 'I'm penniless, is that it?'

'Not quite. There's the marriage settlement. All that comes to you though there's not a great deal in it, I'm afraid. It will, though, help you to carry on. There's Brayne, too, and the prospective sale you told me about. I gather he's interested.'

'I suppose he's genuine,' I said. 'Has he the cash?'

'He has, no question. I've dealt with him before, and had to make inquiries about his finances. He's sound. More than sound. He's loaded.'

'Well, that's something,' Jo said. 'I'll go and see about supper. Help yourselves to drinks.'

'How will you play it tomorrow?' I asked him when she had gone. 'I take it you're coming.'

'Of course. I'll ask for more than will cover the bank, the ACC and the social security stuff so far as I can ascertain it. I don't know how tough he'll be on the deal or if he'll deal at all once he hears the figure. We'll have to play it by ear from there. Jo seems to think he's keen enough to buy.'

'He does seem so,' I said. 'I just wonder why. The place is run down, let's face it—'

'That occurred to me too,' he said. 'But these chaps, you know, if they've decided they want something they catch hold of the bit and go at it, and it doesn't seem to matter much about the condition.'

I still couldn't get it out of my mind that there was something strange at the back of Brayne's apparent eagerness to purchase. It might seem a straight commercial deal to the solicitor, but then he knew nothing about the tape the Colonel had left nor about the O'Shaughnessy connection. I remembered, too, that Bilby Barrows had said he couldn't sell his place to the Yanks, that they only wanted stud farms or leisure centres. Pollardstown might, I supposed, do for them as the first but it would need the hell of a lot of spending on it to make it viable as a stud. But then Davey had said that is what they did. Maybe I was imagining things. But still . . .

'It just seems to me,' I said, 'that he was remarkably quick off the mark and remarkably well-informed. And that meeting with Jo on the steps of the bank was a bit of a coincidence, wasn't it? If he had his eye on the place for reasons of his own, could he have tipped off the bank manager and could the bank manager have talked?'

He gave me a shrewd look. 'Bank managers are not supposed to talk,' he said. 'Which is not saying they don't sometimes. Brayne has a substantial account at that bank. If he's interested and wants the place he could have dropped a word in the manager's ear and, well, a nod is as good as a wink, as they say. And a quick sale would be in the manager's interest too. It'll get him off the hook with his directors.'

'I still would like to know just why he's after it,' I said. 'These guys seldom act out of pure loving kindness, however nice they seem to be. I've seen them in action when I worked on a stud. But you're her solicitor. Is it your opinion that it's in Jo's best interests to sell if the price is right?'

'Look at it this way,' he said. 'If she doesn't sell now the place could hang fire for months, even years. It's not as if it's all that readily saleable as some places are. The title is OK. It's registered land. If we can get a contract signed quickly I'm sure I can persuade the bank manager to ease up on those cheques, especially since the marriage settlement is now at an end. He's not a bad bloke really. He's a bundle of nerves and he's frightened rotten of his directors at the moment over this and his pension, too, I shouldn't wonder.'

'So it's right to sell?'

'It's not only right. It's a gift from the gods.'

All this was going through my mind as we walked up to the iron-studded Gothic doorway of Craddockscourt Castle and pressed the newly-installed brass-mounted bell-push. The door was opened by a pontifical, black-coated butler who conducted us through a vast, domed hall whose black and white floor tiles were immaculately clean and shining. Opening another arched and Gothic door, he ushered us into a library where our feet sank deep into plush carpeting. Books in leather bindings lined the walls behind glass-fronted cases and a gleaming new Waterford chandelier hung from the coved and carved ceiling. Over the fireplace was what looked like an original Munnings and a magnum of champagne stood in a wine cooler on a side table. This was the new Ireland, the Ireland of new money, of the Arab, the American, the entrepreneur and the bloodstock 'industry' from which all pretension of a sport had long since vanished, I thought, as I compared it mentally with poor old Pollardstown, its comfort and shabby chintzes, and Bilby Barrows's blank and boarded-up sad façade. And, by and large, I didn't much care for it. 'How the other half lives,' Davey's quiet voice sounded in my ear as his amused glance surveyed the room. Then the door opened and Brayne came in.

'Champagne,' he said, when he had greeted us and the

butler who had shimmered in behind him had begun opening the magnum, 'or would you prefer it as a cocktail or straight drinks, perhaps—gin and tonic, vodka, there's everything here, I think.'

The butler busied himself sorting out what we wanted and dispensing the drinks. When he had gone we chatted idly in the way one does about the weather and racing in general and whether one would be going to the Curragh for the Derby and where Midsummer Day would run next before the race. Then a door in the panelling, camouflaged by a set of fake books painted on it, opened and the butler announced that luncheon was served.

No one else joined us. O'Shaughnessy, I gathered, was in London, on his own affairs, and checking up on me, I shouldn't wonder, I thought, and where he had seen me before and who I was and what sort of a threat I might be to his own nefarious intentions. Camilla, Brayne said, was in Florida doing something or other with their summer residence there and Jack Manley was not in evidence either, the hired help, as Davey dubbed it, taking their meals elsewhere, away from the quality, I assumed.

Smoked salmon, roast lamb, strawberries, a sort of *bombe surprise* and a massive selection of cheeses followed each other, all served by two maids in uniform under the direction of the butler. We drank Montrachet with the salmon, what seemed to my coarse and uneducated palate to be a superb claret with the lamb and ended up with a velvety vintage port. It was all a far cry from the peeled apple, sliced bread and supermarket cheddar we lunched off at Pollardstown and, I told myself, if the deal didn't go through we'd probably be lucky to get even that. As I did so, I caught Jo's eye and could almost see the same thought passing through her mind. She looked quickly at her plate and groped for her handkerchief to smother what seemed suspiciously like a giggle.

Deciding to make the most of such wines and hospitality as I was unlikely to see again in the immediate future at any rate, I reached for the port decanter which had arrived beside me for the second time and refilled my glass. I had no immediate responsibility for the coming negotiations. Jo and I had already agreed that we trusted Davey implicitly and that we would leave it all to him. He, I noticed, drank sparingly and the port passed him by.

Brayne, there was no doubt about it, was an excellent host. He kept the conversation running smoothly from his place at the head of the table. Yes, Camilla was in Florida and would shortly be going to Fairside, their stud near Lexington, where he was told it was almost unbearably hot; Jack Manley was at the Curragh about some minor problem which had risen concerning Midsummer Day and yes, of course, you had to fancy Midsummer Day for the big one so long as there was not too much give in the ground. Then, turning to me he asked how did I like this weather, it must be a change after the Gulf. I made some non-committal reply and as I did so wondered just how he knew about my sojourn in the Gulf, and then dismissed the thought on the grounds that I was looking for suspicions everywhere since Jo could well have let it drop in conversation. Just the same, I somehow could not rid myself of a slight feeling of unease, the notion that there was something more behind what was happening on the surface here—the pleasant luncheon-party preparatory to a business deal between friends.

I stole another look at him as he leant once more towards Jo on his right. Unquestionably he was a fine-looking chap and he almost exuded niceness. 'No,' he was saying. 'I never hunted. Low goal polo was as far as I got on a horse. But racing and the stud, I love it all. There's something new every year and that brings the thrill of expectation to find out what you've got. Midsummer Day now, he may be the best we've had—' He turned back towards me and to my astonishment I thought I saw something akin to fear flicker for a moment in his eyes. 'There's nothing like the horse to bring people together, is there, Mr Hampton,' he said.

'Or sometimes set them apart,' I said and wasn't quite sure why I said it.

'Yes, there's that too,' he said quietly as he pushed back his chair.

Coffee and liqueurs were served in the library and then Davey looked at his watch, indicating that he thought the time for business was at hand.

'Mr Davey has our entire confidence,' Jo said. 'His family has looked after my family for goodness knows how long. We'll leave everything to him.'

'In that case,' Brayne said, 'we'd perhaps better go to my study, Mr Davey. And perhaps, Jo, you and Mr Hampton would like to see the stud. I'll arrange it.' Without waiting for an answer, as is the way of the rich and confident, he went to a house telephone and gave an order. In a matter of moments we were outside under the porte-cochère where a Chevrolet station-wagon was waiting.

'Well, Dinny,' Jo said to the driver as he turned the car into a side avenue, guided it slowly over ramps and down a slope towards the stud buildings and stallion boxes. 'You're here now, I see. Packed in the riding, have you?'

'Yes, miss,' he said. 'Mr O'Shaughnessy got me the job and Mr Brayne took me on. He's a very nice man, Mr Brayne. He's a divil for building, though.'

The two turreted and battlemented stallion boxes had been retained, I saw, but massive building was going on elsewhere. 'He's converting everything to American style barns,' the driver said as he stopped the station-wagon beside the first of the stallion boxes. 'I dunno but he's right. They all do it nowadays, don't they?'

The usual routine then followed. Stallions and mares were pulled out for our inspection. I've always hated this process. One runs out of complimentary comments pretty quickly and you can't go on repeating, 'There's a lot to like about him (or her)' forever. I remembered with amusement the tongue-tied silences of businessmen owners and visitors to the stud when I had been working there. The only one who had been voluble had been O'Shaughnessy. You could hear him a mile off and, damn him, he'd been usually right. This time I left the talking to Jo who was good at it.

'Where's Hunter's Moon?' she asked when our rounds were, thankfully, nearly finished.

'Over there, miss,' Dinny said, nodding to a box at the end of the shed. 'Sorry we can't have him out for you. He's a bit of a boyo. He's gone a bit fierce-like these days.'

'Is that so,' Jo said, walking towards the box. 'He was like an old sheep before.' She stood for a little while looking in through the grid that enclosed the top half of the door. 'He's certainly got more stallionly,' she said, thoughtfully. Then, as I produced the necessary notes for the tip, she said, 'Thanks, Dinny. No, don't drive us back. We'll walk. I need some exercise after Mr Brayne's hospitality.'

She was frowning as we walked back. I turned to her and said, 'I imagine that you've made me sweat up this hill because there is something you want to say to me about what we have just seen.'

'It's Hunter's Moon,' she said. 'He looks different somehow.'

'Don't stallions always do that as they age?'

'Yes, but it's more than that. I can't really explain it. And there's another thing.'

'What's that?'

'It's Dinny Malone.'

'What about him?'

'He's a crook.'

'What?'

'He was brought up down the road from us. It was the

Colonel who got him his first job in a stable at the Curragh. He was leading apprentice and a bloody good jockey but he couldn't go straight if he was shot out of a gun. If he handed in his licence he was only one jump ahead of the stewards.

'And it was O'Shaughnessy who got him the job,' I said.

'It makes you think, doesn't it?' she said.

By this time we were back at the house and Brayne and Davey were waiting for us.

From their faces I guessed that things had turned out satisfactorily.

'We seem to have reached agreement,' Brayne said, and then, turning to Davey, 'I'll get in touch with my attorney immediately and you'll hear from him.'

We were taking our leave when a car came pelting up the drive. It pulled up beside us and Jack Manley jumped out. 'You seem to be in a great hurry,' Brayne observed mildly. 'Not bad news, I hope.'

'No. It was nothing. I don't know why it was necessary to go at all,' Jack said.

'Bennerton does fuss so,' Brayne said. He was watching Jack amusedly, a faint smile on his lips as he saw Jack's eyes were all for Jo.

As we made a move towards the car in a little group I found Jack beside me. He touched me on the arm and I paused, allowing the others to go on.

'Did you sell?' he said in a low voice, almost a whisper, in my ear.

'It looks as though we did,' I said.

'Don't let her go,' he said. '*Don't—*'

What the devil did he mean? I sought desperately for a means of delaying our departure so that I could learn more. 'By the way,' I said to Brayne, 'what about the horses? Have they been mentioned? There's that three-year-old by Smash Hit—'

'I'm afraid,' he said, rather disarmingly I thought, 'that as I think Dr Johnson said about the countryside, one green field looked to him much as another, so it is with me and judging horses. When I begin to judge a three-year-old it will be my first step into bankruptcy.'

We all laughed at that and saying, 'I leave such things to Francis Aloysius,' he extended an arm as if to usher us to the car. He had, whether by accident or design, effectively thwarted my delaying tactic and there was nothing for it but to make our goodbyes. I was left to go on wondering just what Jack Manley was getting at and what his cryptic message meant.

'Now, Paul,' Jo said once we were in the car. 'Tell us what happened? Is it all fixed? I'm bursting to know.'

'He'll buy all right,' Davey said. 'He's a willing purchaser and he'll pay our price. I've got the heads of the agreement written down. Can it wait till we get back? I'll give you the details then.'

Soon we were again in the Colonel's office. 'We ought to be drinking champagne,' Jo said. 'But the Colonel and I split the last bottle when we won the bumper at Gowran a month or so back with Batman.'

'What happened to him?' I said.

'We sold him. It's what kept us going. Francis Aloysius did the deal. Come on, Paul, let's have the whole thing now.'

Davey took out his notepad, glanced at it as if to refresh his memory and then said, 'It was an easier deal than I expected. I mentioned our price and pointed out that if we didn't get it we'd go to public auction. To my surprise he said snap almost immediately.'

'No horse-dealing?' I said.

'None at all. I don't know, it seemed almost too quick. I got the impression he was a bit on edge and when he'd said yes to the price he seemed to relax. Then he asked were there any other points we should cover. I mentioned to him as you asked me, Jo, if there would be any chance of leaving you in the house.'

'What did he say to that?' Jo said. 'I'm not sure now, but go on—'

'He said he was sorry, much as he would have liked to help he didn't think an arrangement such as that was sound business, and in any event with the new building and general work going on at Craddockscourt he was cramped for room. In fact because of all that he would like to have immediate possession or as soon as could be arranged.'

'What does that mean?' I asked.

'It means that immediately contracts are signed and exchanged he can go into possession here. He must of course lodge the balance of the purchase money on deposit in the names of his solicitor and myself. I told him I'd have to take your instructions and that I'd let him know. Then he said he was intensely sorry for the position Jo found herself in, that he had always liked and respected Colonel Manners and would like to help her in any way he could.'

'Turning her out of her house at a moment's notice doesn't seem much of a way to help,' I said.

'It's not quite like that. He added a sweetener. He said he'd been looking now for some time for a responsible girl to help in his stud in Kentucky. He was sure Jo would fit the bill admirably and he'd be only too anxious to offer her the job if she'd take it.'

'What about a visa or work permit?' Jo asked. 'I've been reading about people being sent back and the trouble there is getting one.'

'I thought of that too and I asked him how he'd get over it. No problem, he said. You can go on a visitor's visa and once there he'll fix it.'

I began to see that there might be more behind Jack Manley's remark than the longings of a lovelorn boy which

I had begun to ascribe it to when thinking it over in the car. But just what was it? I decided I had better see him again and that quickly.

'It's a handsome offer,' I heard Jo saying. 'He's been jolly decent, I must say. It's one solution.'

'Think it over,' Davey said. 'He told me to tell you you had only to phone him tomorrow or any time to go over and discuss details with him.'

'Are there any other snags?' I asked him.

'Not really. The title is all right as I've said. Probate shouldn't take long. There are no undisclosed rights of way, I hope. I had enough of them yesterday.' He gave a short laugh and began to put his papers back into his briefcase.

When he had gone Jo looked at her watch. 'Suppertime,' she said. 'I could whack up an omelette.'

'I'm not hungry,' I said. 'I can't remember when I ate and drank so much at midday.'

'I noticed you were punishing the port.'

'It's not every day I get the chance of sampling a vintage. Never refuse a good offer, and that goes for port as well as horses.'

'And people? I've just been made one or were you so portified you didn't notice?'

'I did and that's why I'm saying let's kick it around a bit. Have you thought about it and do you want to go?'

She took her time about answering, and then, 'I think I do,' she said slowly. It was clear she wanted to say something more and I waited for it. 'You heard what Paul Davey said about our affairs,' she said. 'There's no future for me here, Charles. I can't just hang around trying to use the few pence I have if there are any left, jobbing in indifferent horses and nibbling at the bottle in between. I've seen too many broken-down, left-behind ladies at it—'

'You're pitching it a bit strong,' I said. 'You've a few

years before it comes to that. And there's the Colonel's death. Have you forgotten?'

'No, I haven't forgotten, but—oh, I don't know, I'm almost beginning to think they must all be right, the police and everyone, when they say it was subversives—'

'So you don't want to find out why he left those messages, to know who killed him and why?'

'I don't know what to think, Charles. Too much has happened too quickly. At the beginning I was in shock, I think, and now I don't know whether I'm in shock or out of it. All I feel is that I must get away and it's a wonderful chance. After all, the Colonel's gone and we can't bring him back. And I won't believe that Amory is in any way mixed up in his murder. It's just not possible—'

'I know he seems a nice guy but a man may smile and smile and be a villain. Did you ever hear that?'

'No, and I'm not sure I understand what it means. You've gone all Oxford again.'

'All right, now listen for a second. Jack Manley thinks there's something more than mere kindness behind the offer Brayne has made to you. At least that's how I read what he said to me just as we were leaving Craddockscourt and that's why, I'll wager, he came pelting back from the Curragh in such a hurry this afternoon. "Don't let her go." That's what he said. I couldn't make out what he was driving at. Now I think I know.'

'Jack—he's only a child really. He's well, you know—' She dropped her eyes and smiled briefly and rather shyly.

'I know he's in love with you,' I said. 'There's nothing he'd like better than to get into your knickers but I don't think that explains why he said it. It sounded like a warning to me.'

'Let's leave Jack out of it. Have you any other reason for stopping me going?'

'I can't stop you, you know that, Jo. But if Brayne isn't

mixed up in it, then O'Shaughnessy is—up to the neck, if you ask me.'

She sighed. 'I'm so confused I scarcely know if it's Christmas or Easter,' she said. 'Why do you think that?'

'The Colonel pointed a finger at him and I'm certain it was he who took the page out of Father Milligan's book.'

'But why, Charles, why? Is it to do with the IRA, and if so, doesn't it bring it all back to what the police say it is—a subversive killing?'

'I don't think it has anything to do with subversives. I think the Colonel was trying to tell us something else.'

'If Francis Aloysius is mixed up in something illegal and not the IRA why would he want to conceal his birth? And why did he put it into the Directory anyway?'

'I've thought about that. My guess is that he put it into the Directory because he had to put something in—he's put in precious little else and he thought it unlikely anyone would bother checking it up. Then when he looked at the tape here and found the Colonel was on to his origins he panicked a bit. If he is mixed up with subversives he wouldn't want us to get a lead on him. If he isn't and there's some other reason, it wouldn't do his business any good to have it known he has a revolutionary background. Terrorists or anything to do with them aren't exactly popular with the bloodstock mega-millionaires he mixes with. One way or another he's up to something and the Colonel was beginning to get on to his scent. And let me tell you more—' I recounted to her then, for the first time, my visit from the thug in the flat in London and how that, too, tied in with O'Shaughnessy.

'That still doesn't mean that Amory has anything to do with it,' she said stubbornly.

'True, but there's a damn good chance that he is. They're very thick—thick as thieves, you might say,' I said.

'Just the same, whatever you think I'm going over

tomorrow to see him and find what he offers.' She tilted her chin in the way I knew so well that told me without any words that she had made up her mind and that nothing would change her. I didn't try.

'Very well,' I said. 'That's that, then.'

'And you, Charles,' she said, her tone softening. 'What about you if I do?'

'I'm staying,' I said.

'Why, Charles? It's all so hopeless.'

'Since you ask me, I'll tell you. All these years I was always the odd man out, the useless shit so wet you could shoot snipe off him. Now for the first time one of the family, the head of the family for the matter of that, has had to come to me for help. Me! Can you believe it? I don't suppose you can. Anyway I owe it to myself, which is a silly pompous way of saying it but I can't think of any other. That's why I'm staying.'

We looked at each other in silence for a moment or two, then she stretched out her hand. 'My poor Charles,' she said. 'We haunt you still, don't we?' And then as our fingers touched and she whisked hers away, 'I'll go and whack up that omelette,' she said.

Poor Charles, I thought. It was always thus and ever would be, so it seemed. Well then, let her go to Craddockscourt tomorrow and make her own mind up. For my part I was going to ring Jack Manley to find from him just what he meant by that cryptic warning.

CHAPTER 8

Next morning I saw her depart in the battered old Ford station-wagon which served Pollardstown as a work horse. As soon as she had gone I went in and looked up the

Craddockscourt number in the telephone book. There were two numbers given, one for the castle and the other for the stud and it was the latter which I rang. Someone on the switchboard at the stud answered and when I asked for Mr Manley I was told to wait. After one of those exasperating hangings on to a silent telephone with only the clacking of a typewriter in the background to tell me I was still connected, the voice came back to say it was sorry but Mr Manley was not available. In that case, I said, would he ring me back when he was free. There was a pause at the other end while what I guessed was a murmured consultation took place with a hand over the mouthpiece, since the typewriter noise was now blanked out. Then the voice came on again. It was sorry, it said, but Mr Manley would not be back for some days. He had gone to Newmarket on business for the stud.

'I see,' I said, and replaced the receiver. I thought I did, too. Brayne hadn't missed that whispered conversation and Jack was being kept out of the way.

The next thing that happened was that Jo rang to say she was staying to lunch. In the early afternoon she returned and came into the office where I was playing the Colonel's tape over for the umpteenth time and not gleaning anything from it. She was looking less strained, more relaxed and in a word happier than she had been since this business began. I knew then that she had made up her mind.

'You've decided to go,' I said.

'Yes, Charles, how did you know?'

'One look at you and I could tell.'

'It's even better than I thought. I'm to help getting the yearlings ready.'

'In plain language that means shovelling shit. I suppose you know that.'

'You're pretty horrid. I suppose *you* know that. Do you want to hear the rest?'

'Go on, I'm listening.'

'I'm to help in the office as well.'

'In what capacity? For heaven's sake, Jo, can you spell? You were never a great hand with the pen, as I recall.'

'I took a secretarial course once. Three months of hell in Dublin. It's paying off now. Amory was rather impressed.'

'I'll bet he was.'

'There's a house on the stud I'm to have. They're getting it ready. In the meantime I'm to live in the main house. Camilla will be there.'

'And when does all this happen?'

'As soon as I can. They're short of help. I didn't realize, but Americans don't like working with horses. They're only too anxious to get hold of anyone who knows anything.'

'I see. Jack Manley isn't about. He's gone or been sent to Newmarket.'

'I know. Amory mentioned it. Something about booking a mare.'

'Doesn't that strike you as odd?'

'What? Booking a mare? Of course not.'

'Dammit, Jo, I didn't mean booking a mare. I meant he tried to warn me—us—and now he's been taken out of circulation. It's all too neat—the offer of a job, Jack's being sent off. There's something behind it. If you can't see that you're being wilfully blind.' I knew I was going about this the wrong way, that I should be trying persuasion, that a frontal attack such as this would only harden her resolve, but I couldn't help it, and although I could have kicked myself that didn't help either. Partly I knew now it was that having found her I didn't want to lose her companionship and break the bond, however tenuous, which had sprung up between us; partly it was because I was genuinely frightened for her and knew that once she went there was nothing I could do to help her. Anyway the damage was done, the words had been spoken and could not be taken back.

'You're over-reacting,' she said coldly. 'Do I have to spell it out for you once and for all—I do not believe *Amory. Had. Anything. To. Do. With. The. Colonel's. Murder.* That's my last word on the subject, Charles, and I hope you've taken heed of it.'

With that she went to the door. There she paused. 'You do delight in taking the gilt off the gingerbread, don't you?' she said. 'Still working off that bitterness, aren't you, Charles?'

She closed the door firmly behind her and I was left staring at the blank television screen, feeling a shit and wondering if she was right.

The next few days passed in a whirl. Brayne was as good as his word regarding Jo's visa, which came through quickly, but she was kept busy clearing up and leaving instructions about the horses. The Smash Hit three-year-old had been entered for Tattersalls Derby sale and had been accepted. Cassidy was being kept on for the present at any rate and he would get him ready. The rest, she informed me, were pretty good rubbish—'Tell Cassidy to get what he can.'

As for me I was busy, too, since Davey, hearing of what had been arranged and of Jo's imminent departure for the States, pulled out all the stops and got the necessary papers for probate and the sale moving. I was summoned to his office to approve valuations, check details, some of which had to be referred back to Jo, sign forms and go through the draft contract for the sale of Pollardstown, much of which was double Dutch to me despite Davey's patient explanations and interpolations. All this meant that we had no time to quarrel and anyway I remembered that rows in that family, though often violent, were short-lived. In the meantime I was left to puzzle over how I was to further my investigations, if they could be called that, into the Colonel's murder. I seemed to have run up against a blank wall. All I had were suspicions and no more and I didn't know which way to turn. As it happened, I needn't have worried for events caught up with me, but I didn't know that then.

At last things appeared to have sorted themselves out as well as could be expected. I drove Jo to Shannon airport to catch the plane to Atlanta and thence the shuttle on to Lexington. The rain had gone, the sun shone, the fields had taken on the deep green look which comes to Irish fields after soft rain, and the blue mountains slumbered at the edge of our vision. Among my boyhood favourites from those lonely days in the library at Pollardstown were Somerville and Ross and I remembered their description of such a day as this when 'everything was fit and tense and thin and ready to run for its life like a Derby horse'. At least, I thought that was how they said it, though I knew I hadn't got the quotation quite right. It fitted the day anyway and it wasn't a good sort of day to be leaving behind you to start a new life.

I stole a look at Jo, wondering how she was taking it. She was staring through the windscreen, her thoughts miles away. The Irish countryside, with what someone has rightly called its fierce beauty, has a way of stealing into the hearts of those who live in it and staying there. It had never quite affected me in the way it does those who truly belong to it but I thought I knew something of what she must be feeling. I left her to it and tried to remember the exact words Somerville and Ross had used to describe the day. They ran through my mind in the way a quotation will but I couldn't get them right and in any event only half my mind was on it, for a sense of foreboding which I couldn't shake off had been with me since we started the journey. Then we were through Limerick and running along the wide road across the flatlands leading to the airport.

Shannon airport during the summer months resembles nothing so much as Hieronymus Bosch's idea of hell. It was built as a staging-post and retains all the characteristics of one. When we arrived the check-in hall was as usual occupied by a seething mass of humanity, none of whom appeared to know or to be able to find out which queue they should join. Neither did we, but after several false starts and an interminable wait we fought and struggled our way to a check-in desk which mercifully proved to be the right one.

Then, at last, we were walking down the long corridor and up the stairs to the lobby in front of the glass doors leading to the departure lounge. There we paused. I gave her her hand luggage which I was carrying. Our hands touched as she took it. Then our eyes met.

'Have a good trip,' I said lamely. 'Don't get lost in Atlanta airport and don't talk to any strange men.' Then I added and I didn't quite know why, 'Think of me a little.'

'And you,' she said. 'Miss me a little, will you, Charles? You think I'm running away, don't you? And leaving you to hold the baby?'

'The horse, you mean. The horseholder. That was always my job, or don't you remember? No, I don't think you're running away. You never run away from anything. But keep in touch, Jo.'

'You too. You have the phone number of the stud.'

For once she looked vulnerable. That sense of foreboding which had been with me all the way returned with renewed strength. But I knew her too well to try to influence a last-minute change of mind, however desperately I might wish to do it. I glanced at my watch. 'Time's up,' I said. 'Starter's orders. They'll be boarding in a minute.' I bent to kiss her cheek.

'No, Charles,' she said. 'Not like that. Not like that at all.' Her arms went round my neck. She pulled me towards her and our lips met and kissed and clung. 'Goodbye, Charles,' she said, and then she was gone.

The glory had gone from the day as I drove slowly back along the country roads. Cloud was banking up, darkening the landscape and shutting out the sun. A spatter of rain sprinkled the windscreen. It suited my mood, my sense of loss and the blackness of foreboding which had been with me all day. In the stableyard I found Cassidy, despondency written all over him, standing by one of the boxes. As soon as I pulled up he came across to the car.

'Miss Jo gone, then,' he said. 'Over the water. That's the last of them. We won't be seein' her again, I'm thinkin'.'

'Not for some time anyway,' I said.

'All gone. None of them here any more. And the place sold too.'

'But you're staying on, Cassidy, I understand. Mr Brayne has arranged that, hasn't he?'

'Oh, aye and he's a nice man, Mr Brayne. But there'll be great changes, never fear. It's well for him with all that money to spend. It won't be like the old people. It won't be the same—'

'No,' I said. 'But I suppose it never is—'

At that moment the Craddockscourt Range-Rover swept into the yard. The driver, who was alone, opened the door and got out. It was Francis Aloysius O'Shaughnessy. 'I want to have another look at that Smash Hit three-year-old,' he demanded in his usual brutal, direct way. 'You there,' addressing Cassidy. 'Pull him out.'

Cassidy gave him a look of pure loathing such as only one Irishman from a differing sphere of life can give to another. Then, turning half-about so that his back was to O'Shaughnessy, he shouted, 'Paddy!'

The yard boy must have been hanging about to see what was going on, for he came running. '*Mister* O'Shaughnessy wants to see the Smash Hit three-year-old out,' Cassidy said to him with the first word heavily accented and underlined. 'Bring him out for him.' He then stared ostentatiously at the sky. O'Shaughnessy glowered and I scarcely concealed a grin.

The three-year-old was duly paraded and trotted up and down under O'Shaughnessy's expert eye. He ran a hand along his forelegs, fixed his quarters with an intimidating look and slowly shook his head. 'What's the price?' he said, turning his blank, dealer's stare on me.

'I'm not pricing him,' I said. 'He's in the Derby sale. If you're interested you can bid for him there.'

'I might and I might not. Now I've seen him out I'm not sure I care that much about him.'

Well, damn your impertinence, I thought and searched my mind for something tough enough to say to him. Somerville and Ross came back to my aid once more as I remembered a remark of Mrs Knox in a similar situation. 'I'm not aware that I asked for your opinion,' I said. 'And now that I've got it I don't think much of it.'

I thought he might bridle a bit at that but I should have known he was far too thick-skinned to bridle at anything personal. Instead he gave a guffaw and directed at me a look as much as to say he remembered very well where he had encountered me before. 'You're an odd one,' he said. 'Clever bugger, aren't you? Staying on long here?'

'Just for a bit,' I said. 'While I straighten a few things out.'

He nodded, went off, climbed into the Range-Rover and drove out of the yard. As I watched it disappear under the archway I wondered if that last inquiry had been the real reason for his visit. Cassidy's voice broke into my thoughts. 'That felly,' he said, 'if he told me it was raining I'd go outside to look. He's the sort, Master Charles, as couldn't lie straight in bed. But ye're well able for him.'

'I wish I could be certain of that,' I said.

When I got back to the house the telephone was ringing. I picked up the receiver to find it was Jack Manley at the other end. 'I've just got back,' he said, and then without stopping, 'I've got to see you—urgently.'

'All right,' I said. 'I'm here for the evening. Come along.'

'No. That won't do. I don't want anyone to know we've met.'

'Where are you?'

'I'm in Kilderry. Can you come in and meet me here. I'll tell you where to come. You know Davey's office, don't you?'

'Yes, of course. I ought to, I've been there often enough in the past few days.'

'All right. Up above it, between it and the church there's a street to the left. It's called Oliver Plunkett Street. About half way along there's a pub—Suttons. It's where I'm calling from. Just inside the door there's a snug. I'll be in it and I'll wait for you. It's a quiet place and we can talk.'

CHAPTER 9

I found the pub easily enough. Inside, it was a piece of Victoriana, all brass fittings and mahogany counters, polished and gleaming. The only occupants, so far as I could see, were two serious drinkers sitting on stools at one end of the long bar, crouched over pints and conversing in low tones. The snug was on the left of the entrance. It was a small panelled affair in which a table and three chairs took up most of the floor space. On its walls were a faded photogravure print of Golden Miller and a brighter one of Arkle.

Jack Manley was sitting facing the door, an evening paper open at the racing page on the table in front of him. 'What'll you drink,' he said as I came in. 'Whisky?'

I nodded and he banged on a hatch behind him. It opened and a head poked through. 'Whisky, Dan,' he said. 'Scotch. Better make it a large one.' The drink came and the hatch was closed. He pushed the glass across the table towards me, saying as he did so: 'You let her go. I tried to warn you. Why—'

I wasn't in the mood to be lectured by Jack Manley. 'You try stopping her when her mind is made up,' I said. 'She takes hold of the bit and that's it. Now what's this all about?'

'She's going to be in trouble,' he said. 'Big trouble and you've got to get her out of it. I can't.'

'Suppose you tell me why and how,' I said.

He took very little notice of that but went on as if I hadn't spoken. 'They're up to something,' he said. 'They're frightened. They don't know how much you and she know or have guessed—'

'Has this anything to do with the Colonel's murder?' I said.

'I think so. I looked after Dick at the end when the cash had run out and he knew he was going to lose the place and was drinking himself silly. They had something to do with that, so though they took me on I don't exactly love them. I knew my way about the old place and heard them talking when they didn't know I was there. They wanted Colonel Manners out of the way and now they want her out of the way, and you too.'

I felt the hairs on the back of my neck bristle. Things were ever so little beginning to fall into place and the place they fell into wasn't nice. 'It's O'Shaughnessy, isn't it?' I said. 'He's behind it?'

'That bastard. He's not a man, he's a monster. And he's in with the mob. He's got some hold over Brayne. They were having a row one day and I heard him say to Brayne as if he was threatening him, "If that old Frenchwoman talks—" then I came in and they shut up.'

'What about Brayne? I'm told he's the original Mr Clean.'

'Mr Clean! You must be joking. Did anyone who ever made all the money quick as he did keep himself all that clean? And he's had a face lift and a nose job. Did you know that?'

'No, but that doesn't necessarily make him a crook,' I said mildly.

'Maybe not. But the purchase of Pollardstown was set up. I heard him on the phone talking to the bank manager, and the manager tipped him off when Jo was coming in that day he met her on the steps of the bank. They've got a secret somewhere. Colonel Manners was on to it and they think you may be too and they're scared shitless—'

'Have you any idea what it is?'

'I dunno. It may be something to do with Midsummer Day. They've gone for gold on that colt. They said they weren't running him at Epsom because they thought the Curragh would suit him better. That's all balls. He was stopped in his work before the Derby and they didn't want it known. They took him out and now everything is riding on the big one at the Curragh. I hope he breaks his bloody neck. God, how I hate the bastards.'

'If you hate them so much,' I said, 'why do you stay on? I've always been told that if you're good with horses they never let you down. You could get a job anywhere.'

'I don't know,' he said sulkily, looking away from me and then staring down at his drink, but suddenly I knew why. It was because of Jo. He wanted to be near her. Poor young man, I thought. He wasn't up to her weight and never would be. His next words told me I was right. 'I'm frightened for Jo,' he said. 'Once she is there, in America, she's in their hands. She's on a holiday visa, isn't she?'

'That's right. Brayne said he'd get her a JI, whatever that is.'

'It's permission to work for eighteen months, a sort of step before getting the green card, the work permit.'

'Well then, what are you worrying about, that's all right.'

'Like hell it is. I'll tell you what happened to me, why I can't go back. I was working on a stud on a tourist visa, just as she is. I was sent in to phone a message to some government department, I forget which, it doesn't matter. The nosey bitch at the other end snapped at me and when I told her where she got off, "Do I detect a foreign accent," is what she said and put down the phone. Next thing I knew the immigration bully boys arrived. I was slapped into handcuffs and carted off to the slammer along with a lot of Mex who were rounded up at the same time. No one stood bail for me—it costs a bomb—and after being half starved in that bloody slammer I was chucked on to a train bound for the State pen along with the load of crappy Mex. It's no joyride, let me tell you. The guards on that train are so tough they eat their boots for breakfast, strange things can happen and no questions asked. You're stateless, and hopeless and helpless.'

'But,' I said, 'Brayne said he'd regularize things once she got there.'

'Can't you see, for Christ's sake? He's no intention of doing it. One anonymous telephone call to immigration and they'll snap her up and once she's on the train she's a non-person. I know. I've been there. No one wants you, no one knows you, they can do what they like with you. If you get to the state pen it's not much better—'

'You survived,' I said.

'I survived. Most of the Mex did too, for that matter. They don't give a damn. When they're shipped home they wait a bit and then walk back across the Rio Grande and they're in again. And I was lucky, no one was gunning for me and they were shipping a batch back soon after I arrived. But that state pen—I saw enough to know that anything goes, male rape is about the best of it. There were no women on our trip but I heard stories—' He shivered at the recollection and took a gulp at his drink.

'Just what are you trying to tell me,' I said, half appalled by his story and half not believing it.

'If she gets on that train she won't arrive and if by any chance she does she won't come out of it—'

I looked at him doubtfully, wondering if he wasn't exaggerating, if his feeling for Jo had not led him into wild imaginings, and yet—he'd been there.

'Are you quite sure—' I began hesitatingly.

'Why the hell do you think I brought you here if I wasn't sure?' he interrupted me. 'They murdered Colonel Manners, didn't they? Or if they didn't they were behind it, like I said. One call to immigration and she'll be on that train. Then . . .' He left the rest unsaid.

'But,' I said, 'in God's name, why?'

'I wish I knew. It's to do with Midsummer Day, I'll bet. There's something damned odd about that colt.'

'Don't be so sure it's the colt. Jo originally thought it might have to do with the Colonel's time in SOE. That was a cloak and dagger outfit he was mixed up with in the war. And Barrows thought it might be too. And there's that threat you heard—"If that old Frenchwoman talks". I still can't understand, though, how Brayne got himself mixed up in it, whatever it is. The Colonel liked him, Jo likes him and will hear nothing against him, Barrows says he's liked in racing, come to that I rather liked him myself, what little I saw of him.'

'Brayne isn't the worst of them, I'll give you that,' he said grudgingly. 'But that bastard O'Shaughnessy has him over a barrel somehow. I don't know what he has on him.'

'"If that old Frenchwoman talks,"' I said again. 'What the devil does that mean?'

'Search me. But I think there is something foreign about him. It's a sort of trick of speech. It mightn't mean anything, but I've an aunt married to a Frenchman who has lived mostly in England. Sometimes Brayne's voice, his way of saying things, reminds me of him.'

'Where does he come from originally? How did he get into racing?'

'I don't know all that much. No one really asks any questions in racing about your background, do they? It's your money, and your horses they're interested in. But he had a place in Vermont, I believe, and then like lots of the rich he decided to go into bloodstock. He bought the Fairside Stud in Kentucky. It was over the purchase of the stud that O'Shaughnessy first got mixed up with him. But damn them, anyway. It's Jo I'm thinking of. You'll get her out of there, won't you?'

'I'll try,' I said, though as of that moment I hadn't a notion of how I was going to do it.

'I can't go back,' he said. 'But you can and you can get there now without a visa from some of the places in England.'

I pushed my chair back. 'Keep in touch,' I said. 'And keep your ear to the ground.'

'Take care,' he said. 'And watch your back. They'll be after you too and sooner rather than later, I shouldn't wonder.'

Driving back, my mind was in a turmoil. Was what Jack had said true or was he, because of his feelings for Jo, wildly over-reacting? Somehow I didn't think he was. What he had said and his manner of saying it had the ring of truth, and that was reinforced by O'Shaughnessy's visit that afternoon and his sounding out how long I was likely to stay. There was, too, that attack on me in the flat. They might be up to something more serious now.

The first thing I did on my return to Pollardstown was to go to the Colonel's desk, open the secret drawer and take out the Luger. It was probably a capital offence in this country or something near it to be in possession of a lethal weapon without a licence. Well, that was a risk I'd have to take; the Colonel had said it might come in useful and he could be right at that. I slapped one of the magazines into the butt and worked the action to put a round into the breech. At the same time I felt pretty silly standing there with an automatic pistol loaded and ready to fire in my hand. I had to keep reminding myself that this might be the twentieth century but that bits of it were as raw and rough as the jungle and that a murder had taken place in the room where I stood.

The old house seemed to sense my mood of apprehension. Its ancient timbers creaked and groaned and the wind which had got up had an eerie whistle to it. As dusk came on I drew the curtains and felt a little less naked, but the sense of foreboding was still with me. There was no point in trying to make the house secure. I didn't suppose there was a window or door in the whole place which wasn't an invitation to an intruder. That didn't help much to reassure me. I watched the news on television, which concerned itself entirely with disaster home and abroad and close-ups of advanced obstetrics. The weather, it appeared, would be unsettled. I went to bed.

There was no lock on the bedroom door, or rather, there was one but it had lost its key which in any event had not been turned in living memory. I left it open the better to hear and be warned early of any intruding noises, pushed the Luger underneath my pillow feeling a bit comforted by its presence, read Adam Lindsay Gordon which I found beside my bed, resolved to sleep with one eye open, and turned off the light.

In fact I did drop off more heavily than I intended and I don't know how long I slept. It was the sound of voices which woke me. I lay on for some minutes, immobile in the bed, listening. At first I could not believe it, that there were people in the house talking, loudly and without concealment, and I thought I must still be dreaming. I wasn't, though. It was no dream and no hallucination either. The voices came up quite clearly from downstairs. Even by straining my ears I could not make out what they were saying but that they were there, unauthorized and unasked, was clear enough. Taking the Luger, I slipped out of bed.

The landing was empty. A pale moon had come up and was shining through the tall window whose curtains had not been drawn since the last servants left. At the head of the stairs I could hear the voices more clearly and moreover see where they were coming from. A rectangle of light flowed from the open door of the dining-room into the hall and whoever owned them were in there. They grew louder. It seemed as though they were arguing. I took the Luger off safe and made for the stairs.

It was the moonlight and, I suppose, some sort of sixth sense which saved me. Something caught my eye as I looked down at the first tread of the stairs. Stretched across it about six inches from the carpet was a taut, thin nylon cord. In that instant I saw it all. It was a nicely baited trap. They reckoned I'd come rushing out to investigate the voices, trip over the wire, turn base over apex, tumble down and break my neck. Or if I didn't a quick bang on the head from one of them as I lay at the bottom would complete the job. Remove the wire and leave me lying there and then trot off to collect the blood money from whoever employed them and it didn't take much guessing to know who that was—O'Shaughnessy without a doubt. No questions would be asked—and why should they? It was just another tragic accident. Sad business over there at Pollardstown. Sad place, that. Lightning strikes twice. Cause of death bad luck. Perhaps he'd had a drop too much, poor fellow. Write it off.

Moving very slowly, I stepped over the trip-wire. Going down, I kept close to the banisters. I had crept up those stairs too often in my boyhood, anxious to avoid waking the Colonel and incurring his wrath when I had been out later than I should have been, not to know how to miss out the steps that creaked. It was as well that I proceeded cautiously. Careful chaps, those who laid the trap. They evidently believed in the belt and braces technique. Three steps down was another wire. I missed out that one too.

Reaching the bottom, I skirted round the rectangle of light and looked into the room.

Two men were sitting on either side of the long mahogany dining table. Behind them the French window through which they must have come stood open. A standard lamp had been turned on near the door. It was that which was casting its light into the hall as an inducement for me to investigate, I supposed. Save for it, the room was in shadow.

Between the two men was a pack of cards with what looked like an ugly black cosh lying on the table beside it. They were wearing gargoyle masks, one of a clown, the other of a satyr. Together with the muted light and the shadows in the long room the whole effect was both sinister and frightening. The masks muffled their voices but I could now make out what they were saying.

'Why the hell doesn't he come?' the clown was asking as he took a card from the pack.

'He will,' the satyr answered. 'Getting jumpy, are you? Shout or scream or something, then. That should bring him.'

'The big guy told us it'd be a pushover. I hope he's right.

I just wish to hell we'd hear him moving. I don't like this place. It's creepy. It gives me the shits—'

'All right then, scream. Pretend you're being raped. That'll be the day. What's that—?'

There was a sound from behind them at the window. They both turned to look. A figure had suddenly materialized out of the night and was standing in the opening. 'Jesus, Mary and Joseph,' a voice said. 'Holy Mother of God, what's going on here?' It was Cassidy on his lonely rounds, something they hadn't allowed for. He stood, staring appalled at the masked faces turned towards him.

It was my opportunity and I took it. I stepped into the light and raised the Luger. 'As you see, gentlemen,' I said. 'I'm here already. Now take off those silly masks and let's have a look at you—'

'He's got a gun,' the clown said in a sort of high whine. 'We weren't warned—'

'Shut your trap,' came from the satyr.

Then several things happened simultaneously. With the speed of a striking snake one of the satyr's hands went to the cosh, the other swept the standard lamp aside. It turned over with a crash and plunged the room into darkness.

The cosh same sailing through the air and took me on the side of the head, knocking me off-balance. As I fell the Luger jumped in my hand and went off. Damn these hair triggers, I thought stupidly as I heard a yelp of pain. Then there were more crashings and bangings as furniture overturned, a shout from Cassidy followed by hurried footsteps—and silence.

Feeling more than a bit foolish and with a singing in my ear where the cosh had taken me, I picked myself up off the floor and groped my way to the light switch. Pressing it down, I saw Cassidy sprawled by the window. For an awful moment I thought I had shot him and it was with unutterable relief that I saw him clamber slowly to his feet.

'Saints and sinners defend us,' he said. 'I thought it was the divil himself had come among us. And you with the gun.' He sat heavily down in a chair. 'Glory be to God, Master Charles, what devilment is happening here now?'

'I have an idea they were intending to do me in,' I said. 'You may have arrived just in time. I think I winged one of them. Thank God it wasn't you I hit. Are you all right, Cassidy?'

'I am that. If the Colonel's horses couldn't break me up the likes of them fellahs won't.'

'I'll get us a drink,' I said. 'I think we both need one.' Going into the kitchen, I brewed up some coffee and found a whisky bottle. When I placed it on the table I saw that Cassidy had followed me in and I pushed the bottle towards him. He filled the best part of half a tumbler and waved away the water jug.

'One thing me father taught me,' he said. 'Never waste good whisky on water.'

Reaction was beginning to set in. I found myself shaking and reached for the bottle. Cassidy had got down a good half of his drink in one gulp. He swallowed, wiped his lips and looked across the table at me. Then he picked up his glass and finished the drink. I pushed the bottle towards him again. The whisky and, I supposed, the events of the night had loosened his tongue.

'Times, terrible times,' he said. 'And they gave you a bad time, too, when you was growin' up, Master Charles. Why did ye come back at all?'

'I don't think I quite know,' I said. 'Maybe it was because the Colonel asked me. He left me a letter—'

'Aye, I know, 'twas a way he had. I was with him, man and boy, thirty years. I started here at fourteen as a yard boy. He was a hard man, the Colonel. Always got what he wanted, he did. The only time he didn't was when things were goin' badly at the end and the trouble there was, whatever it was, between him and Mr Brayne.'

I had only been listening with half an ear. I was still in some sort of shock, I think, and I was cursing myself for having let the Luger off. I might well have killed someone, Cassidy in fact if it came to that, and it was damn lucky I hadn't. I reckoned that scream or squeal I'd heard came from one of the hired assassins and had been more from fright than anything else. Now, hearing what Cassidy was saying, I suddenly sat up.

'Something between him and Mr Brayne?' I said. 'What was that, Cassidy?'

'I heard them arguin' like once in the yard a month or so back. The Colonel was sayin' something to Mr Brayne, I didn't catch what it was but Mr Brayne, he didn't like it, he was put out. I heard him clear enough. He sort of shouted, "No, no, you're quite wrong," and he got into his car and drove off and I never saw him again until after the Colonel died and he bought the place and that's the truth of it.'

'You didn't catch what the Colonel was saying to him? You're sure?'

'That I am. Will ye be gettin' the Garda after this night's work?'

'No, Cassidy, I won't, and I don't fancy those intruders will, either. We'll leave the Garda out of it unless someone could have heard the shot and reported it.' I might be in trouble then, I thought, with the unlicensed Luger.

'Report, is it?' Cassidy said. 'They'll not do that. If they heard it at all, which I'm thinkin' no one did, they'll close their ears or say it was someone shootin' rabbits. Well, perhaps I will have another drop, Master Charles, thankin' you.'

Cassidy was becoming expansive. After he had refilled his glass he stared ruminatively at the bottle. 'D'ye know what it is,' he said. 'They do say the best thing ye can do with a bottle of whisky is to throw away the cork. Take the Colonel, now, he was never a man to do that. Never a great one for givin', the Colonel. The only words that ever passed between us were about the wages when they went up. I knew him better nor anyone else since the mistress died. And Master Mike bein' killed, he took that terrible hard. After that he got a bit sharp-like with everyone, and he hated them new racin' stewards, he was always either cursin' them or laughin' at them and that didn't help him with the horses. He was terrible hard on people, them that didn't measure up, as he used to say.'

'And was Mr Brayne one of them?'

'Aye. He found out somethin' about Mr Brayne that made him change his mind about him, I'll be bound.' By this time Cassidy was on his feet and by the door. He looked steadily at me. 'Ye shouldn't have come back, Master Charles,' he said. 'Good night to ye.' He went out and I heard his footsteps echoing down the passage to the garden door.

CHAPTER 10

Whisky and coffee mixed are not really good antidotes to shock and Cassidy's parting words did little to quiet my racing mind. I kicked and twisted in bed for what was left of the night. It was clear to me now that both Jo and I were under threat and a violent one at that. How close it was to Jo I could not guess. If Jack was right and their plan was to ship her off as an undesirable alien or an illegal immigrant or whatever they called it, they were hardly likely to do so immediately since that might call attention to them. On the other hand, might they not indeed act quickly if they wanted us both out of the way in a hurry? So my mind jumped about and ran on. It did seem that I should assume the worst and act on it and that meant getting Jo out of there in a hurry—but how? I'd have to persuade her first of all that she was in peril and that might take some doing. To say the least of it, she hadn't been kindly disposed to my efforts to dissuade her from going at all. And I had little enough now to add to what I had said then except the attack on me in the night and what Jack had said. She might well answer me that the first had nothing to do with her and that Jack was letting his imagination run away with him.

So my racing thoughts ran on. Well and good, I said to myself, she might indeed dig in her heels and say no but I still had to try. Jack had said I'd have to go and get her and it looked as though he might be right. At all events, the first thing to do was to ring her up.

By this time I was finishing my breakfast and I was about to reach for the phone when I remembered that we were five hours in front of the US and whatever hope I had of persuading her was unlikely to be improved if I brought her to the phone in the early hours of the morning. But the more I thought about it, the more certain I became that I would go. I had to face the fact, too, that I wanted to see her again —and badly. I was missing her, that was the truth of it. I didn't like myself much for this and I didn't like her much for it either. I knew too that there was no future in it but it didn't make any difference. It was just another fact I'd have to face.

But there were things to be attended to before I went. First I must get in touch with the solicitor to see if there were any difficulties arising in the estate which would demand my presence or immediate attention.

'No problem,' he said when I was put through to him. 'The papers have all been filed and if any queries arise that I can't answer I'll get in touch. Leave me an address—'

'I'm not sure about that yet,' I said. 'I may be moving around. I'll let you know as soon as I can. How is the sale going?'

'The contract, as you know, has been signed. The requisitions on title haven't come in yet, but I don't anticipate any difficulty.'

'One thing,' I said, and I had intended to ask it from the first since my view of Amory Brayne was changing. 'Brayne's money is all right you say. Have you any idea where it came from?'

I held my breath for his reply since it might, it just might, give me some clue as to what was behind it all.

'He was an analytical chemist, I believe,' he said. 'He patented some sort of pill or potion, I don't know the exact details, and one of the conglomerates, having heard about it from a spy of theirs, bought it up for a huge sum.'

'He took the money and ran.'

'More or less, but it wasn't quite as simple as that. When the conglomerate were about to put it on the market they found from experiments it was producing some woeful side effects. You know in America now litigants can sue for a cut finger and recover millions. They had quickly to whip it off. There was talk of their suing Brayne but nothing came of it. They'd bought it with their eyes open, so to speak.'

'How do you know all this, Paul?'

'I have a cousin in the business. He told me. And that didn't stop him, you know. He's made another couple of fortunes since, one with bottled water containing a cure-all, I'm told.'

'I could do with some of that right now.'

'Try some if you're thirsty or put it in your whisky. Sorry to cut this short but I've someone coming in on the other line.'

An analytical chemist. So that's where Brayne's money came from. It gave me something to think about, if not much. And at that moment the green Renault van which brought the post drove past the window.

There were several letters addressed to Jo, most of them bills, and one to me in a hand I didn't recognize. Opening it, I turned to the signature to find it was from Denzil Colton.

Dear Charles [I read],

I don't know if you're still interested in what happened to your guardian and SOE, but as promised I mentioned it to Pa between glasses of port (he's run out of vintage and is now on late bottled or vintage-style. I think it has improved his temper). It's given him something to think about apart from his bank manager and his wine merchant. He sprang into action immediately. As it happens, he does know something about that operation which went wrong. It seems there was a leak somewhere. Anyway he's been poring over old maps and diaries and he's got a library about SOE. And he's kept in touch with such of his old pals as are left and haven't fallen off the perch. He'll tell you what he knows about it if you can catch him early enough in the day. If you're back in this country I think you should see him. He lives in a commuter cottage in Little Finchley, which in case you didn't know is in darkest Gloucestershire. Phone me and I'll go with you. I like to keep an eye on the old boy occasionally.

I read it again. However faintly, I seemed to be making progress in unravelling the skein of mystery and for that matter mayhem which the Colonel and the manner of his death seemed to have spun around Jo and me. I didn't like it much; I'd never cast myself as a hero but I was into this thing now, whatever it was and whether I liked it or not, and if I didn't break it someone was going to break me and very nastily too in view of what had happened already. In other words, I had to get them before they got me. I was doing no good here and if I was to catch one of those visa-free flights to America and Jo it meant being in England. I could fit in a visit to Gloucestershire on the way. That having been decided, I rang Denzil and caught him in. Yes, he said, he was free and would accompany me to Gloucestershire tomorrow. His father, he said, was all agog to talk. I packed a bag and went outside to say goodbye to Cassidy.

'Ye're right to go,' Cassidy said as he shook my hand. 'There's nothing for ye here, Master Charles, and the place sold and the horses, what's left of them, going. I've looked after things before and I'll do it again. God be with ye.'

'I hope he may be. I may need him,' I said. Then I pulled out the Porsche, and drove like the wind, or rather, as fast as I was able, taking no risks, to Rosslare.

I made the night boat, snatched a couple of hours' uneasy sleep in a hard chair, drove on through the night and arrived back at the flat in good time to ring Denzil. He'd come round straight away, he said.

Little Finchley, when we got there, proved to be rather as Denzil had implied in his letter, a sort of advertisement for yuppiedom. It looked like a Hollywood film set for Ye Olde English village. The green was mown and cropped, the inn sign 'Ye Jolly Potman'—could that be original?—gleamed with fresh paint, as did the windows and doors of the houses round about and their window-boxes vied with each other in colourful display. 'No yokels in smocks?' I said. 'Perhaps they're only here at weekends too when they're dancing round the maypole.' There was a Bentley Mulsanne outside a bigger house opposite us. This was the only sign of life in the place. I assumed its owner had taken the Lamborghini to London to give it a run.

Denzil indicated a house in one corner and as I pulled up he explained rather apologetically that 'all this'—and he waved his hand at it—had happened long after his father had come here on his retirement some time in the early 'fifties.

Brigadier Colton proved to be a stocky man of medium height wearing a crew-necked pullover with the shirt collar open over it. He was almost entirely bald and his cheeks bore a formidable array of battered and broken blood-vessels. He had a pair of brown eyes and they weren't the soft, feminine, appealing brown, they were hard like tan leather and male. He didn't look in the least senile to me. 'I usually take a glass of port at this time,' were his first words. 'Perhaps you'll join me.'

A full decanter stood on a side table and without waiting for an answer he produced three glasses. 'Now then,' he said. 'You want to know what happened to poor Tom Manners in that operation of his which was all fucked up. Come over here.' He led the way to a table in the window. On it was one of those large-scale French ordnance maps of Béarn and the mountains near the Spanish border. 'I was in the area myself for a bit,' he said. 'Refreshed my memories looking at this map. Looked up some old diaries and books; talked to a few chaps, those that are left. See here—' He stabbed a stubby forefinger at a point on the map.

Leaning over, I saw where his finger was indicating. A series of zigzag white lines led upwards through the contours. They appeared to peter out high up in the mountains to be followed by a dotted line that too ended where the words *Fort du Marigny* were printed.

'It was a Napoleonic fort,' the Brigadier explained. 'Built in a hurry when they thought Wellington might come that way out of Spain. He didn't, of course. He went further south. It fell into disrepair and was reactivated in the middle of the century when there were rumours of deteriorating relations with Spain. Some sort of care and maintenance garrison was left there on and off and it was used as a training base for mountain warfare, I believe, until the last war and the occupation of the whole of France. The Boche got it then and made it a base for guarding and sealing the escape routes into Spain. The Gestapo were in charge. They brought captured Resistance chaps there and tortured them far away from interference, or so they thought.' He paused, took a sip of his drink and stared in silence at the map, reliving old memories, I imagined.

'Was the Colonel, that's what we always called him, taken there?' I said, breaking into his reverie.

'No, he wasn't, but one of the Maquis he was working with was, a leader, a chap they called Renard, the fox, many of them had these false names, you know. If he'd talked, and the Gestapo had ways of making the toughest talk, he'd deliver the whole network into their hands. They resolved to get him out.'

'Some undertaking,' Denzil said. 'I know those mountains. I've skied there and we did an exercise with the French there once.'

'As you say,' the Brigadier went on. 'But they had one advantage. The Germans were constantly carrying out repairs to the fort which by that time was pretty well falling to pieces. It was towards the end of the war, the second front had started and they were short of manpower. They press-ganged some of the locals into doing the work. The Resistance infiltrated a couple of their chaps into the working party.'

'Did they all come from the area?' Denzil asked.

'Yes, they swept them up from the villages. There are a lot of them about on the lower slopes, little mediæval huddles of houses, most of them. You must remember them, Denzil, if you were there. Anyway, to continue, there was a sort of outer gallery leading to a gun position, the retaining wall of which had collapsed. That was what the workers were first set to repair. Well, the Resistance managed it that the work would be badly done and a place left weak—weak enough for a storming party to get through. Meanwhile another section under Tom were to mount a diversionary attack on the fort from above so as to distract attention from the raiders below who had plans of the interior and where Renard was held. The infiltrators had seen to that.'

'What happened?' I asked quietly.

'It didn't work. When the raiding party went in the Gestapo were waiting for them. Tom's party, too, were ambushed and virtually wiped out.'

'Someone talked,' Denzil said.

'Yes, but who?' the Brigadier demanded. 'It was thought that Renard to whom news of the raid was smuggled in might have been broken under torture but he was later shot with those who were taken prisoner.'

'And the Colonel's party?' I said.

'Wiped out almost to a man. There were only three survivors: Tom Manners, who was hit, and two others, one of whom was wounded too. They managed to get across the Spanish border where a family in the mountains took them in. The wounded chap died, Tom survived as did the other but he was killed in a car smash soon after the end of the war.'

'So the Colonel was the only one who knew anything, if anyone did?'

'Not quite. There was talk that the traitor was known in the area but he escaped.'

'The Colonel never went back.'

'Not so far as I know. Your guardian was a disappointed man. He regarded himself as a failure. He was bitter over his sacking in the desert and he blamed himself for the cock-up of that operation and losing his men—quite wrongly, in my opinion. He retired to Ireland and buried himself there with his horses.'

I was certainly learning things about the Colonel I had

never dreamt of. 'I'm only a simple soldier,' had been one of his sayings. I could see now that he must have been mocking himself as he said it.

'It's all so long ago,' Denzil said.

'Is it?' the Brigadier said. 'I suppose it is to you young fellers. It seems like yesterday to me. But there it is. That's the story as I know it.'

'Someone knows more,' I said slowly. 'Or I think they do and what you've told me makes me more certain. But what and where the connection is, that's the puzzle.'

'I see,' the Brigadier said. 'Or rather, I don't. I'm in the dark. Perhaps now you'll tell me what all this is about.'

I told them both in detail and they listened attentively. 'Of course,' I ended, 'it may all be a false trail.'

'I don't think so,' the Brigadier said. 'Something's afoot. Tom Manners was killed because he knew something. And they think he may have told you and that girl, your cousin, what he knew. If she's with those people in America you'd better get her out of there. Is there anything else?'

'Well, yes,' I said, suddenly remembering. 'There is. It's not much but Jack Manley, he's a sort of general dogsbody of theirs, heard them having a row and there was one thing he heard O'Shaughnessy say which he thought might be significant and so do I now. "If that old Frenchwoman talks," was what O'Shaughnessy said and Manley thought he was threatening Brayne when he said it.'

The Brigadier frowned. '"If that old Frenchwoman talks,"' he repeated. 'D'you know, that rings some sort of a bell. There was talk, I remember, of an aristocratic Frenchwoman—or was it a nun? No, that was somewhere else. One of the penalties of old age is lack of memory for names. I wish—No, it's no good. Come in to lunch, maybe it will come back to me.'

We trooped into a modern kitchen complete with eating alcove and benches. An elderly body was bustling about with dishes at the cooker. She looked fondly at the Brigadier and suspiciously at the port decanter he brought with him. 'The vino, Denzil,' he commanded. 'It's in that cupboard there, or should be if Mrs Harkness here hasn't finished it.' He glared at her. 'Now, no nonsense, Mrs H.,' he said. 'I like a glass of wine with my lunch and, damme, I'm going to have it and these young men, too.'

It was an Orvieto which I supposed he'd got a taste for in Italy, and by the time we had finished a very good soufflé, a ripe stilton and the port I noticed that his eyelids were beginning to droop and his head to nod. When we returned to the living-room he sat himself carefully in a chair, yawned once and went quietly to sleep. We left him gently snoring.

'You look knackered,' Denzil said to me when we got outside.

'Do you wonder?' I said. 'I've been up all night and drinking port all day. And trying to think through what I've been told.'

'I've always wanted to drive one of these things,' he said, opening the offside door of the Porsche and getting in behind the wheel. 'I'll take it home. I reckon it'd be safer.'

Of course he drove far better and far faster than I did. He wasn't over-horsed; he was part of the car and the car obeyed him. He drove on the tachometer; the changes went in like butter and the needle stayed steady. There was no jerk or sudden application of brake, no hesitation and his line on corners never deviated an inch.

I dozed for a bit while he threaded the country roads. Once we were on the motorway we slid along the fast lane at a hundred with only the whisper of the tyres to betray our speed. My mind was still on the conversation with the Brigadier as I fought off sleep. 'I thought you said your father was senile,' I said. 'He didn't seem that way to me.'

'Boredom,' he said. 'You've given him an interest, a new lease of life, you might say. His war wound is at him all the time, and although you wouldn't see it his eyes bother him so he can't drive much. That means he can't go racing, which was one of his passions. He won the Foxhunter's at Liverpool before the war. Most of his friends have fallen off the perch, too, so he's lonely and has no one to talk to except that old biddy who wants to marry him. So he has nothing to do except drink port and live in the past reading the memoirs of the Generals he served with and didn't think much of, most of them.'

'Is he likely to remember anything more about the Frenchwoman?'

'He'll try, anyway. As I've said, it's all given him something to think about. And he liked you, I could see. That'll help. He doesn't like everybody. I'll keep pushing him, if he needs it.'

By this time we had arrived back at the flat and he came in for a quick drink. With it in his hand he wandered over to the window and stood by the curtain, very still, looking out.

'I wish I knew where the whole thing was going,' I said. 'It's like a bad dream. Sometimes I wonder if I'm going to wake up.'

'They've tried to hurt you once and kill you once, whoever they are. It's real enough. Looks like they may try again.'

'Thanks for those kind words,' I said.

'You're impaled on what in our schooldays we were taught to call Morton's Fork, aren't you?' he said. 'You have to go on because you're damned if you do and damned if you don't.'

'On a hiding to nothing, in fact?'

'That's about it. But the old boy was right. The first thing to do is to get that girl out of there.'

'Point made and taken. What are you staring at? Have another drink and sit down.'

'You were asleep and didn't notice it but we were followed when we left Little Finchley. The guy couldn't drive very well and he hadn't the power under him I had. That's why I had to go a bit faster than I liked. I lost him. But it occurred to me he might have picked us up again and be hanging about.'

'And is he?'

'Not so far as I can see, but if he's a professional I probably wouldn't anyway. You have a very distinctive car. If I were you I'd check it before you drive it again. A pound of semtex is a good one-way ticket to eternity. Thanks for the drink. I'm supposed to be meeting Trevor Haig, the trainer, at the Ritz. Good night.'

'I hope it isn't goodbye,' I said as the door closed behind him.

When he had gone I did a mental calculation of the time factor. We were five hours ahead of America. That being so, I thought I might catch Jo at the stud and I did. But it didn't turn out to be a successful call since she wasn't forthcoming, to say the least. 'I can't talk to you now,' she said. 'I'll ring you back as soon as I can.' I told her I'd left Pollardstown and was in London at the flat. 'It may be a little while before I get back to you,' she said when I gave her the number. 'Stick around.' And that was that.

There wasn't any food in the flat and I didn't feel like going out and foraging for a meal; besides, she had said to wait for her call and I didn't want to risk missing it. I fixed myself a drink and went back to my chair. As I sipped I felt drowsiness creep over me. After all, I'd had very little sleep for two nights. My eyes closed and I slid into slumber.

The shrilling of the phone woke me. For a moment I didn't know where I was. Then realization came and I grabbed it. It was Jo.

'How are you?' I said sleepily. 'Are you all right?' The moment I said it I thought what a bloody silly thing to say and that I'd get a smart answer that would singe my ears. To my surprise I didn't.

'Ye-es,' she said hesitatingly. 'Things are different. It's pretty strange—'

'I've heard that. Sort of they order things better—'

'Listen, Charles,' she said, cutting me short. 'I'm not at the stud. I'm in Hennigan's. It's a place where all the Irish go, a kind of club for them. I didn't want to ring from Fairside. I've a horrid feeling I'm being watched and I think I might be listened in to. Francis Aloysius has been sniffing around here too. He's gone now but Camilla's here. She's well, but she's edgy—'

'What's up with her?' I said.

'I don't think I know. She keeps looking at me when she thinks I don't see her, and it's all the time as if she's on the point of telling me something and then changes her mind. And she's worried about Amory. I don't know how many times she's asked me how he is and how he looks and how he seems. She was worse when Francis Aloysius was here.'

'Who wouldn't be?'

'There's that but there's more than that. It's not very nice, Charles.'

This was all unlike Jo. She sounded unsure of herself and as near as nothing to being frightened. 'What's with you, Charles?' she went on. 'Why are you in London?'

'Things have happened here too,' I said. 'I'll tell you when I see you. Look, Jo, I think I'd better come out.'

'Oh, Charles, would you—'

'I never thought I'd live to hear you say that.'

'Shut up, damn you, I'm thinking.'

'That's more like my old Jo.'

'You'll want a car. Come to Hennigan's and I'll meet you there. Don't ring the stud. Ring here and they'll take a message to say what day and time you'll arrive. I'll leave instructions how to get here at the car hire desk at the airport. It's beside the guy who has a sporting art gallery. I'd better go. Apart from everything else this is costing a bomb. Looking forward, Charles—'

So that, for the moment, was that.

I was shaving next morning when the telephone rang. Thinking it might be Jo again I picked it up quickly. It wasn't Jo, it was Denzil Colton. 'I thought I should get hold of you immediately before you set off on your travels,' he said. 'You've certainly set my old man's mind, what's left of it, working. He got me out of bed an hour ago to tell me he's remembered the name of that Frenchwoman he thinks they might be referring to. Not a nun, you'll be surprised to hear, far from it.'

'Who was she, then?'

'Hang on a minute, I've got it written down. Here it is —Louise Lavallière. He's remembered all about her, too. He's thrilled to bits about it. Says it brings back old times. Anyway she and her husband came down from Occupied France and took over a near-derelict château at a place called L'Esté in the Basses-Pyrénées—'

'Look, Denzil,' I said, 'I'd better take notes, I've got a pad somewhere.' I pushed some of the foam off my face, found a pad and a ballpoint and sat down by the phone.

'They set about restoring the château,' Denzil went on. 'The husband died soon after the Occupation but she carried on. She was the hell of a good-looking woman, Pa says. Very soon she was up to her neck in the Resistance. But she was clever. She played both sides. She'd be entertaining Gestapo officers to dinner while guys on the run or escapers would be laughing their heads off upstairs in the attics or outside in the stables. She was believed to be sleeping with the Gestapo boss and getting the low-down on their doings across the pillows. Pa doesn't know if this is true or not.'

'Is she still alive?'

'She must be if it's the same woman they were talking about, mustn't she? It's a long shot but it's worth a try. There's a bit more if you are interested.'

'Of course I am. Go on.'

'At the end of the war there was the hell of a lot of jealousy and recriminations and accusations of collaboration flew about. Someone got hold of the story of her sleeping with the Gestapo boss and informed on her. There was talk of her being brought to trial. Pa doesn't think it ever came to anything, but she was apparently ostracized in some quarters. Pa doesn't know if she's still in the château but she might be. There it is, anyway. He said I was to tell that nice young fellow I'd brought with me yesterday, he'd forgotten your name. That's how it is with geriatrics. They can't remember last week, only fifty years back.'

'Thanks, Denzil, and thank him for me, will you?'

'For nothing. He's enjoying it. If he comes up with anything else I'll let you know. Where will you be?'

'At a pub called Hennigan's outside Lexington, Kentucky, in the Blue Grass—if I get there,' I said.

CHAPTER 11

Hennigan's was a large bare room with chairs and tables dotted about. There were coloured photographs of The Minstrel and Secretariat on the walls, together with the Keeneland set of Peter Williams prints. Across one end a long bar stretched the width of the room The place was empty when I got there save for a barman polishing glasses. I ordered a gin and tonic and watched with some fascination as he filled a glass with ice, poured in gin and added a whisper of tonic. It was my first experience of the American way of mixing drinks. When it came it tasted mostly of ice-water, which was just as well as it was blindingly hot outside.

I'd taken a flight with Delta to Atlanta, taking advantage of the visa-free scheme for visitors, and then made my way on to Lexington. It had all been done on credit cards without leaving the flat, for after Denzil's warning I had an uneasy feeling that I might be watched.

There was a back entrance to the flats used for bringing in coal and suchlike. To gain it, you went through a portion of the old basement, across the cellars and down a narrow passageway. I used it for my departure and picked up a taxi to take me to the airport, leaving the Porsche where Denzil had parked it on our return from seeing his father.

As I paid for the drink the table rocked uneasily on its legs. The barman swore gently under his breath, took a bar mat from another table and rammed it underneath the offending leg, which sagged ominously. 'Gets a bit boisterous here nights, sometimes,' he said. 'You from the old country?'

'In a manner of speaking, yes,' I said, and at that moment Jo came through the door. She glanced quickly round the room as I rose and beckoned her. Then she sat down opposite me and we looked at each other.

'Well—' she said.

'Well then—' I said, and we burst out laughing together.

'I think I'm homesick, Charles,' she said. 'It's all so strange—that's one reason the Irish congregate together here.'

'And when you're homesick I know any old familiar face will do—like me,' I said.

She gave me a level gaze out of her grey eyes. 'You can put it that way if you like,' she said and looked away.

'I think I'd better tell you what's been happening,' I said quickly, breaking the constraint which had suddenly sprung up between us. And I did, keeping it as undramatic and low key as I could.

She listened without interruption—that was one thing about Jo, she was always a good listener, it came from living so much with the Colonel, I supposed—her chin on her hand she watched me as I spoke. When I had finished she raised her eyes to mine. 'All right,' she said. 'I believe you now, but before we decide what to do next I've something to tell you. Camilla has warmed up a bit.'

'Oh, and what has she to say?'

'She's frightened out of her mind for Amory. She knows there's something dreadful going on but she doesn't know what it is. He's told her not to come back to Craddockscourt for the present and she's more or less admitted that she's been instructed to keep an eye on me to see that I don't step out of line.'

'And Francis Aloysius is behind it all?'

'Well, yes. She says everything was all right until he came into their lives. She's sure he has a hold over Amory and that it's something out of the past.'

'It looks as though she's dead right there.'

'She said she had found something which might—just—throw some light on it. I told her that you were coming out. Perhaps I shouldn't, but I didn't know then what you have told me now. She thinks you may be able to help and wants you to come to dinner tonight. It's all so awful. What are we to do, Charles?'

'I'll tell you when I've seen Camilla,' I said.

Our way to the main house took us through the stud. A driveway between rows of mature beech with acres upon acres of rolling stud-railed pasture stretching away on either side brought us to a stone-built bridge over an ornamental lake. Beyond was a graceful cut-stone building with a spire and a weathercock. A fountain played in front of it and a wide Roman archway gave entrance to it. 'What's that?' I asked her.

'It's the stallion barn,' she told me.

'Forgive me, I thought it was a cathedral,' I said. 'What's he got there now?'

'Nothing much, to tell the truth. Sansovino, but he's getting old, Tippecanoe who won the Preakness but he hasn't come up to expectations. Woodmansterne, they've just got him and I don't know much about him. All their hopes just at the moment seem centred on Hunter's Moon and he's at Craddockstown, as you know.'

'Just where is Francis Aloysius now? Not here, I hope.'

'He's in Japan but he's been here, as I told you. I don't think I was supposed to know. I imagine he was checking up on me. Anyway I was told someone was sick and I was sent to one of the faraway barns, but a redneck saw him driving away and told me.'

'What the devil is he doing in Japan?'

'Looking for another cheap one he can bring back and turn into a prodigy like Hunter's Moon, I suppose. You know, Charles, I can't help thinking there's something fishy about that stallion. They wouldn't bring him out that day we were there. And that Dinny Malone they've brought in as stud-groom to look after him, he's a right little crook. And there's that business about him being savage. I told you, remember, he was like an old sheep when he was racing.'

'Stallions change, though, don't they? Maybe he hasn't had enough mares. That's what's made him savage. Happens to humans too.'

'Missing your houris of the desert, are you? I thought if you got up to any tricks with those they cut your hands off?'

'If that's all they cut off you're lucky.'

'Seriously though, Charles, I'm wondering if they've got hold of a ringer.'

'You can put that out of your mind. The days of switching stallions which used to go on in studs, and not fly-by-night ones either, you'd be surprised, are past since the lodging of blood samples came in. Don't ask me why and I've never understood it, but their blood is not like humans'. Every horse's blood is different, almost like a human fingerprint. So that nice little racket has been stopped.'

'Oh well, it was a thought. I suppose birds of a feather and crooks to crooks and all that and that's why he got Dinny. Here we are, turn left and mind the ramp.'

The house was a rambling clapboard mansion with a centre block and a verandah supported by graceful iron pillars. We went under this through a glass-fronted door into a long cool hall carpeted with oriental rugs. On the walls were not the sporting prints I had expected but modern Impressionists.

Camilla Hurbury was waiting for us. She was tall and handsome and moved with a lithe grace. Her brown hair was flecked with grey; she had an oval face, flawless skin, dark lustrous eyes and a mouth which looked severe until it suddenly sprang into a smile. I could see immediately why she had captured Amory and kept him for so long. 'I've heard about you,' she said to me as she extended a hand in greeting. 'Let me get you a drink, or perhaps you'd open the champagne. It's a small art, isn't it, and one I've never tried to master.'

We dined in an airy room with the sun flooding through the lattices. She kept the conversation flowing easily. We talked of hunting in Ireland and Virginia where she had been brought up, and of horses and races and personalities. Inevitably the name of Francis Aloysius came up. It was when the servants had gone and brandies had been set before us. 'I have to say,' she said, 'I cannot take to him.'

'You put it mildly,' I said, 'and believe me, you speak for all of us.'

That seemed to clear the air and allowed her to talk without constraint. 'Then I'll say frankly, Charles,' she said, 'and here it is: nothing has been the same since he became racing adviser to Amory. I am sure now that he has some hold over Amory and it is making his life a hell. And I don't know what it is.'

'Didn't he ever give you any hint of what it could be?' I asked her.

'No. Never. I daren't ask outright. If I even approach the subject he turns it away. All I know is that it is getting worse, as if it's approaching a climax.'

I knew I had to question her and I knew I had to tread carefully in my questioning. I felt that she had guessed or learnt something more than she had yet revealed and that she was so tortured with worry for Amory that she longed to divulge it but that she had to trust us before she would. 'Forgive my asking this,' I said, 'but is it something out of the past?'

'I forgive you, Charles,' she said. 'You must ask anything you think will help.'

Once more I hesitated. I remembered the Brigadier's story of betrayal and death. If Amory had had a hand in that his secret would be dark indeed. But could this be, for he seemed far too young and, moreover, there were as yet no links with him. But still . . .

'If,' I said tentatively, 'and I don't for a moment say it, but if by any chance it turned out to be something discreditable—'

She turned those lustrous eyes on me. 'I love Amory, Charles,' she said simply. 'Every man, especially a successful man, has something in his past he is far from proud of. Amory is sensitive, perhaps hypersensitive. He would be only too susceptible to such pressures as Francis Aloysius would try to bring. I can't think or believe that whatever it is is very bad. In any event, whatever it is I don't care. Nothing could be worse than the way we are. I'll do anything, anything,' she repeated, 'to get that devil off his back.'

'Have you any idea—' I began.

'I know what you are going to ask,' she said. 'What do I know of Amory's past, his origins. The answer is nothing. He was at Harvard. I do know that. But he has always avoided anything in the nature of a probe into where he came from before that or how he got there. Amory is an even-tempered man, Charles, but it is the one thing I know which can deeply disturb him and he will show it. He doesn't erupt or storm as some do. He sinks into an impenetrable silence which can last for hours or even days. I have learnt not to cause these bouts of utter withdrawal. This much, though, I do know and that is that he was brought to this country many years ago by a relative.'

'How many years ago would that be?' I said, doing a mental calculation back to the war. 'And how old is he now?'

'I don't know,' she said surprisingly. 'But I have found something which may give a clue to some of the questions you are asking and which I ask myself. I'll show you.' She rose and crossed to a bureau in a corner. Opening a drawer, she took out a photo in a silver frame and brought it over to us. The glass of the frame was cracked but the photograph was clear to be seen. It was the head and shoulders of a beautiful woman in a white blouse staring coolly at the camera. 'It has always stood on a table in his dressing-room,' she said. 'He has never told me who she is and I have never dared to ask for the reasons I have explained. A day or two back I was in his dressing-room fetching something he had asked for on the telephone and quite by accident I knocked it over. It fell and broke and the back came loose. I have replaced what was there. Open it, Charles.'

I slid the catches up and freed the back. Between it and the photograph was a postcard which fell on to the table in front of me. It was a picture-postcard in full colour of a massive building against a background of mountain and sky. Across the top were printed the words *Fort du Marigny*. At the very bottom a gallery ran and in its centre was a large inked cross.

'Turn it over,' Camilla said.

When I did so I saw printed in large inked letters similar to the cross on its face the single word REMEMBER. The photograph was lying face downward on the table and I saw that on its back was written in a firm sloping hand *With all my love—L.*

'Madame Louise Lavallière,' I breathed. 'And the fort must be where the Colonel's Resistance party was wiped out. So there is a connection—'

'You're speaking in riddles,' Camilla said. 'Obviously you know something. You must tell me—'

I looked at her. She was sitting leaning forward, her long fingers twisting together again and again. She too, I thought, was living with the sag and strain of nerves. 'Jo's father, Colonel Manners, who was as well my guardian,' I said, 'was liaison officer with a Resistance party, one of whose leaders was captured and held in that fort. They mounted an operation to rescue him. It failed.' And I told her as best I could what Brigadier Colton had told me.

'But how could Amory have been involved?' she said. 'He's too young.'

'It's what I thought too,' I said, and even as I said it I remembered Jack Manley's mention of his having had a face lift. That might or might not be true. Jack's imagination, I thought, was a vivid one and coloured by his dislike of his employers, but on the other hand much of what he had warned me about appeared to be turning out all too accurate. 'But the key to the secret is there or thereabouts,' I said. 'It must be.'

'But who could have sent that postcard?' Jo said.

I looked again at it. There was no postmark. 'It must have come in an envelope,' I said. 'And it's been there some time. How long is it since Francis Aloysius took over Amory's racing affairs?'

'Some years back,' Camilla said. 'It's hard to say exactly. He's gradually come to have greater and greater influence and now it's almost as if he owns the horses and Amory too.'

'Louise Lavallière,' I said. 'If she's alive she must know what happened at the Fort.'

Camilla poured more brandy. 'He used to get letters from France,' she said. 'He never told me what they were or who they were from. Latterly I think they've stopped. Oh, Charles, what can we do?'

'Find Madame Lavallière for starters,' I said.

'And just how do you propose to do that?' Jo said.

'By going to the Basses-Pyrénées if that's what they're called,' I said. 'And the sooner we start the better.'

CHAPTER 12

We caught the small twin-engined shuttle to Atlanta. There we found there were seats on the Paris plane and, thanks again to credit cards, we were able to take them. Before we descended to the underground railway that would take us to international departures Jo went off to the loo and I searched for a paper. Finding a *New York Times* on a rack, I bought it.

Glancing through it, a paragraph tucked away at the

bottom of a page caught my eye. Bomb in London, I read, and, reading on:

> At Clayhanger Street yesterday a bomb explosion destroyed a Porsche car and killed its occupant, presently unidentified. The owner is believed to be abroad and the police theory is an attempt was made to steal the car resulting in the death of the thief. Approximately 1½ lbs of Semtex explosive was used. No organization has claimed responsibility for the outrage, which appears to have been motiveless or a mistake.

Mistake, my foot, I thought. That bomb was meant for me. Denzil's warnings had been all too accurate and a miserable car thief had copped it instead of the intended—me. It was a near miss and too damn near for my liking. Putting the paper under my arm, I ran for the phone.

I got through almost immediately but it was Denzil's answering service which came on. For a moment I had panic that it was Denzil who had been blown up but I dismissed it immediately. Had it been, he would have been named; besides, if he had been the victim someone would be manning his phone and it would not be his answering service I'd be talking to. 'Listen, Denzil,' I said into it. 'I've just read about the Porsche. You were right and they're getting closer. I'm in Atlanta, Georgia. I've extracted Jo and we're about to take off for Paris, France, and Pau in the Pyrénées. I'm sure now O'Shaughnessy is behind it all. If we don't come back in a week or so have a stern word with him, will you?'

Jo was standing beside me when I hung up. 'Where did you get to?' she said. 'I've been looking all over. And who on earth have you been gassing to? If we don't get going we'll have missed the plane.'

'Read that,' I said, handing her the paper and pointing

to the paragraph about the Porsche. 'That's my car. Someone has started to play very rough indeed. What the hell are they hiding?'

'One thing anyway,' she said to me as we sat in the rail-car being whirled along through the bowels of the earth. 'No one knows where we are or what we are going to do.'

'Except Camilla,' I said. 'I wish now I hadn't said that about the Basses-Pyrénées.'

'She won't talk. She hates Francis Aloysius as much as we do.'

'They'll have ways of making her, threatening Amory more than likely. They're up to something big whatever it is and we're in it, like it or not. We've just got to find Madame Lavallière.'

'If she's alive.'

'She'd better be, so keep your fingers crossed.'

We made the Paris plane with not much to spare and then caught the bus from Charles de Gaulle to Orly and there we waited, snatching what sleep we could on the airport seats until it was time to leave for Pau. We landed on time but it was raining, driving in gusts across the tarmac as we made our way to the airport buildings.

However hard I tried and thought, I had very little better idea than Jo had of where we were going or what we were to do when we got there. All I knew was that it was vital to put as much time and space as quickly as possible between ourselves and those likely to be hunting us. I felt certain that Louise Lavallière was the key to the whole thing if only we could find her. If only—

At all events what first we had to do was to hire a car at the airport and this—credit cards again—presented no problem. In Pau I found my way more by luck than good judgement to the Avenue de Pyrénées. Clouds were now obscuring the much vaunted view, big, black, sinister clouds which were banking up all around and the rain had turned into heavy drops which hit the roof of the car with soft thuds. Storm was in the air.

Leaving the Avenue, I turned into the Place Royale, found a parking place and went in search of a Michelin map. When I returned we crossed the road to the café on the opposite side. I ordered cognac, which was about the only French I knew and which I thought we needed. When the drinks came I unfolded the map and together we pored over it.

'There it is,' I said pointing. 'L'Esté. The château must be nearby. We can easily make it tonight. It is simple enough; we go out that red road N. 134. Then through Oloron. Then after about ten miles there's a white road leading to L'Esté. There, see, we can't miss it.'

She seemed strangely subdued. 'I hope you're right, Charles,' she said. 'I suppose I'm to do the map-reading while you sit behind the wheel and curse me.'

'Something like that,' I said.

'Very well, just for that I'll have another of these drinks —' She laid a finger on her glass. 'God, just look at that rain.'

It was coming down in solid sheets now, spattering off the pavement outside, running in rivulets down the gutters, and over the hills I thought I saw a flicker of lightning.

'Nice evening for a drink and a chat,' she said as we ran across the Place to where we had parked the car. 'Where are you preparing to stay, Charles? With the lady in the château? She's hardly likely to put us up, is she? And time is marching on in case you hadn't noticed it. What's more, these clothes and I are getting a bit tired of each other after this trip you've taken me on.'

'There must be a pub in L'Esté if all comes to all,' I said.

'That's what I was thinking, oddly enough,' she said enigmatically, leaving me to work that one out.

In the deluge it took me several boss shots, one of which brought us straight back to our starting point, to get out of the city, all due to her bad map-reading as I reminded her, but the first part of our trip went easily enough. Then things began to go wrong.

After Oloron, which we got through with only a minor hiccup and a near miss with a camion at a roundabout at the entrance to the town which gave her an opportunity to comment sweetly on my driving, we commenced to climb and it was then that the storm really hit us. First there was that low rumble which presages approaching thunder, then the rain intensified so that even with the wipers at full stretch I could hardly see. In front of us so far as I could make out everything was obscured by a deep black cloud. Suddenly this was split in two by a brilliant flash of lightning which lit up the whole landscape of rock and scree. This was followed almost immediately by an almighty crash of thunder. It rolled away reverberating through the hills, to be succeeded by an even more vivid flash and an explosion directly overhead which actually rocked the little car.

'That was a near one,' Jo remarked as she pored over the map which the flash had illuminated. 'What next? What now?'

Ahead of us was a road to the right leading apparently further into the hills. 'I think that may be the white road you spoke of coming up,' Jo said uncertainly. 'But I'm not sure and if you curse me I'll curse back.'

'We'd better take it anyway,' I said. 'God alone knows where we are and this storm may be even puzzling him.' I changed down and turned into it. After about a hundred yards it began to corkscrew upwards and at the same time the rain and the storm intensified if that were possible.

It didn't take me long to realize that we were wrong. The contours on the map when I had examined it in Pau did not indicate any upward spiral and here we were climbing all the time through what seemed a never-ending series of hairpins. The road narrowed too so that there was no chance of stopping to turn back even if the storm had allowed it.

The sheet lightning was now interspersed with jagged flashes of fork and from what I could see there was beside me a sheer drop to which I didn't dare give a second look. It was all I could do to hold the car on the road, negotiating those damned hairpins and keep on keeping on until we arrived somewhere or the road petered out, which I hoped most devoutly it didn't.

Jo was bent over the map, reading it as best she could in the flashes which illuminated the whole wild country about us as if it were daylight. 'Don't swear at me, Charles,' she said. 'But I think I've got it right this time. There should be a village of sorts somewhere ahead.'

'I'm too busy to swear,' I said, and then, suddenly, in the light of another flash I saw a cluster of buildings set up high above us on a spur of rock. 'You've got it this time,' I said. 'Houses ahead.'

Two more climbing hairpins on which we slithered and scrabbled, putting my heart into my mouth, led us to a narrow street hardly wide enough to admit the car. The street was set on a steep slope which the rain had turned into a running river that swished from our wheels as we climbed upwards. Grey stone houses were piled one on another up the slope. Shuttered and silent, they frowned down on us as we climbed. There was no sign of life. There wouldn't be, of course, in that storm and it was getting late. The inhabitants would be well battened down, probably praying; I felt rather that way myself. At length we reached the top of the street which gave on to a little square. In front of us, incongruously, a sign in white letters on a blue background and a pointing arrow indicated PARKING. I followed the arrow into an empty space. It was a sort of wide platform and directly in front of us in the headlights we could see a large square house with, over the door, the sign HOTEL.

The storm had abated a bit or moved on, for it was flickering over the far mountains, but the rain was still pelting down. 'Succour seems to be at hand,' I said, pulling on the handbrake. Congratulations on your map-reading.'

'That's a change if you mean it, which I doubt,' she said. 'If I'm right, this place is called Bersse and it's right in the heart of the hills however we got here.'

Leaving the car, I ran to the hotel door. It was shut but on an upper panel was a big brass knocker in the shape of a bear's head. Seizing this, I banged it down. Nothing happened. After waiting a minute or two I took hold of it again and beat a tattoo. Still there was silence within. Water was beginning to drip inside my collar. I was about to repeat the operation and create a rat-tat-tando on the knocker when I heard footsteps approaching. There was the rattle of a retaining chain being withdrawn and the door opened. A youngish guy of about my own age or a bit older stood there. '*Fermé*,' he said briefly. '*Nous sommes fermés*.'

I groped for what schoolboy French I had, which was precious little. My mind had gone blank in the way it does at those moments and I was getting wetter by the minute. In despair I spluttered out: '*Parlez-vous anglais?*'

He shook his head. '*Non, m'sieu*,' he said and repeated, '*Nous sommes fermés*.'

Suddenly Jo appeared beside me. She had evidently heard the exchange and sized up the situation. To my amazement she addressed the guy in what seemed to me at any rate to be the most fluent French.

At first he shook his head but she persisted, imploring and gesticulating and pointing to the weather and our wet clothes. He weakened then a little and allowed us to step in while she continued her sob story of stranded travellers in the storm, and in about two minutes I thought she would cry on his shoulder. We advanced a few steps further in. 'He can hardly throw us out now,' she said in an aside to me, 'and don't you start getting John Bullish and shouting at him. I'll handle this.'

'Where did you learn to speak French?' I said.

'At that secretarial course from a tape. I'll explain later.'

In the end he relented. Jo's *beaux yeux* if those are the right words, her pleading, her feminine wiles and command of the language all turned the trick. He had one room, he said. He smiled, looked at both of us, shrugged his shoulders and led the way up a curving tiled staircase. At the top he threw open a door, switched on a light and stood aside for us to enter.

It was a large airy room with a partitioned-off bathroom in one corner. There were two easy chairs, an uninviting horsehair chaise-longue, and a luscious-looking double bed against a wall between two tall, curtained windows. I looked at that bed and began to mouth with difficulty the few words of French I had been rehearsing on the way up. '*Avez-vous une autre chambre?*' I said. '*C'est ma sœur—*'

He looked at me and then looked at Jo. Then he raised his eyebrows slightly and shrugged his shoulders again. '*Non, m'sieu,*' he said. '*Je regrette . . .*' He looked at Jo again, a faint smile appeared on his lips and he left the room.

'And now what are you playing at?' Jo inquired acidly as the door shut behind him. 'I'm not your sister in case you didn't know, or couldn't you remember the French for cousin.'

'Once or twice removed,' I said. 'He didn't believe me anyway and, let's face it, dear, just in these circumstances you don't look like anyone's sister—'

'Well! Is that intended to be an insult or a compliment? Whatever it is, and just for that, you can go and forage for something to eat and drink. I'm going to get out of these clothes as quick as I can and have a bath.' She was moving towards the bathroom as she spoke and pulling her jersey over her head. 'So get moving, chum.'

With the prospect of a night on that damn chaise-longue in front of me I decided to concentrate more on the drink than anything else. I needed it too after that drive. Finding *le patron*, as I took him to be, in the bar, leaning on the counter and doing his accounts, I made my needs known to him by a mixture of fractured French and sign language. Wearing what I can only describe as a sort of conspiratorial grin, he produced an unlabelled bottle of red wine which he explained came from his own vines, he had no whisky, he said, but when I spotted a bottle of *crême de menthe* on a shelf behind him he reached up and placed it before me with another of his knowing grins which I could have done without.

Food was more difficult. It appeared there was nothing in the house. He fell silent for a moment as if in thought and then went off through a door at the back of the bar. In a few moments he returned bearing a tray on which were wine glasses, a large round, ripe Brie, a plate of butter and four long French rolls. Thanking him profusely as best I could, I put the bottles on the tray and made for the stairs. '*Bon appétit*,' he said to me as I left. '*Bonne nuit—et le reste.*'

When I returned to the room Jo was standing by an occasional table she had pulled out from a corner, belting her dressing-gown about her. We ate the Brie, our hunger spiced by our adventure on the road, and drank the wine which was ripe and fruity and as good as *le patron* had promised. But a sort of constraint had sprung up between us. The spectre of that damn chaise-longue seemed to hang over the meal.

'Byron said a woman should never be seen eating or drinking unless it be lobster salad or champagne,' I said, as much to break the silence as anything else. 'And, like a lot of what Byron said, it makes better sound than sense.'

'Still quoting, still showing off, Charles?' she said.

'No,' I said. 'I'm not showing off, but if you like to change the subject you said you'd tell me how and when you learnt to jabber in French.'

'It was at that secretarial course. There were tapes there and we could take a language as an extra. I had the idea the Colonel wasn't going too well financially and I thought another language might come in useful some day.'

'It has. I'm learning new things about you every minute.'

She looked me squarely in the eye. 'Are you?' she said. 'I wonder . . .'

Reaching over, I opened the *crême de menthe*. 'Tart's tipple,' she said as I poured. 'That's what the Colonel used to call it.'

'We always seem to come back to him,' I said. 'Odd, isn't it, how he played such a part in all we did. He overshadowed our lives and the lives of others, it now seems, too.'

'Too many, too much maybe,' she said, and then, abruptly, taking her glass. 'I'm going to finish this in bed. Your turn at the tub.'

When I came out she was sitting up, sipping her drink, her hair a sort of halo around her, regarding me steadfastly. The chaise-longue was empty of either pillows or bedclothes of any sort. I felt like kicking it and stood there looking at it.

'Well,' she said. 'Come on. What are you waiting for? There's room for two.'

'If you say so.'

Thankfully I clambered in. She was right; there was plenty of room; the bed was about the size of a boudoir. She reached out and snapped off the light. Velvety darkness enfolded us. I could hear her light breathing beside me; she hadn't settled to sleep; neither for that matter had I. Suddenly she spoke. 'Charles,' she said.

'Yes.'

'Charles. I'm—I'm frightened.'

'You know something?'

'What?'

'I'll tell you. So am I.'

'Are we ever going to get out of this awful tangle the Colonel has landed us into?'

'We'll get out of it. The opera isn't over until the fat lady sings. Always remember that.' I wish I believed just that but she'd done so well so far I wasn't going to let her down now.

'Oh, Charles, I only wish we knew where she was or what song she'd sing. Oh, Charles—'

Her hand slid across the sheet and touched mine. Our fingers intertwined, and then, I don't know, it seemed the most natural thing in the world, we were in each other's arms. Somehow she had slipped her nightdress off. Her skin was like silk and she came to me with an abandon I could never have guessed at. The soft darkness and our fears and our need heightened the instant we made love almost desperately, two fond and frightened people, and the climax came. Afterwards as we lay there spent she reached up to touch my cheek. 'You never guessed, did you?' she said. 'You wouldn't allow yourself to believe it, would you, but I've fancied you ever since we were teenagers, ever since you arrived, I think. Why do you imagine I saved that picture for you from Mike, why do you think I teased you on the stairs the day after we came back from London?'

'But you were so tough and glamorous and good at things—'

'Were we? I wonder. Mike, maybe. He inherited that hard streak of the Colonel's and the Colonel was determined, I think I see now, to have him make up for all his own disappointments and nothing much else mattered. You know, I never really liked Mike. And he hated you. I think he was afraid with your brains you might some day take some of the notice away from him. Mike had always to be the tops. Why didn't you stand up for yourself and hit back at us?'

'What? With the three of you riding me and telling me how useless I was, what in hell could I do?'

'I wasn't riding you.'

'It didn't look that way to me then. Wet enough to shoot snipe off—I'll never forget that. It wasn't until I got away that I began to make something of myself. I read somewhere recently that it's all balls to say a man ever outlives his boyhood. Maybe it's true.'

'You read too many books. Try reading people for a change. You never read me, that's for sure. Oh, Charles—'

And then we were making love again, quietly, companionably this time, as if we had been waiting for it all our lives as perhaps, in a way, we had.

And then, afterwards, I fell into a dreamless sleep. When I woke it was morning. I put out my hand towards her but the bed was empty. Opening my eyes, I saw that the curtains were drawn and the sun was streaming through the windows. She was standing by them, looking out. Hearing me move she turned around. 'Come over here and look,' she said.

Slipping out from under the tousled sheets I joined her. What we saw was worth looking at. The hotel had been built on the very edge of the mountain shelf. Below us the ground fell sheer away to the floor of the valley. Opposite were the tree-clad slopes of another mountain which climbed up through rocky outcrops to a towering peak where snow still lingered. To our left was a cleft in the hills along which the road we must have traversed in the storm curved and climbed. Little white houses like child's toys carelessly thrown dotted the lower slopes. The storm had long since gone. The air was pure and clear.

My lips brushed her cheek. 'It's not a bad place for us to have found each other,' I said.

'It's magic,' she said. 'If it wasn't for this awful nightmare we're in.'

'Remember—' I said.

'I know,' she cut me short. 'Wait until the fat lady sings.' She laughed and raised her lips to mine.

Downstairs we showed the map to the patron when we paid his bill. In the storm we had taken a road too soon, he said. L'Esté was in the next valley and we should have no trouble finding it. Jo explained our errand to him and he frowned. 'But Madame Lavallière is no longer there,' he said. After the war, he went on, she remained in the château for a little while and then she had gone away, to America, he believed, and had handed it over to the state. The house was now an art and folk museum and the grounds and gardens were open to the public.

'Oh, Lord—' I said to Jo, 'another dead end.'

Then, seeing, I suppose, the look of disappointment on my face, he added: 'But do not despair. She came back, though not to the château. There were several old retainers left and kept on. One or two of them will surely be still there. They may well know of her whereabouts.'

CHAPTER 13

The valley which we turned into after leaving the hotel was as unlike the one we had left as it well could be. A gentle slope led us down to a corner which plunged us into a beech forest. Here great trees grew thickly about the narrow road, in places meeting overhead forming a sort of tunnel through which the sun came dappling. After a mile or so it began to climb and then, suddenly, it ended.

We emerged into a bowl among the hills which stood around on every side. In front was a cluster of houses and directly facing us two wrought-iron gates guarded the entrance to the château. These stood open and we went up a short drive flanked by cut and cropped beech hedges and so came to the house itself. Creeper-clad with a high mansard roof and tall, symmetrical white-painted windows, it was hauntingly beautiful as it gazed serenely across its shaven lawns and clipped box borders.

I parked with other cars on a gravel side-sweep where an arrow directed us to the office. There a girl behind a table with a roll of tickets and a rack of picture-postcards on it told us that the next tour of the house would not start for three-quarters of an hour. When we explained who we were looking for she frowned and shook her head. 'I am not from here but from Pau,' she said. 'And this is my first year here. But wait . . .' She left the table and went into an inner room, returning after a few minutes with an older woman. She, too, shook her head. No, she said. There were none of the former employees left, unless . . . she spoke rapidly to the girl and I caught the name 'Aristide'. There was, so it seemed, as Jo explained to me, just one remaining, Aristide Déjour, the last under-gardener of the former régime of the Lavallières. He was very old and *très difficile* but if we liked we could try with him. He might remember her, he might know where she was living, she had the name of being very loyal and kind to her old employees. Apart from that she knew nothing for she, too, was a stranger, she came from Tarbes. Aristide might, just, be willing to talk to us, then again, if he was having one of his bad days . . . She raised her eyebrows and opened her hands expressively. But if we cared to try we should find him in the garden. He still pottered around and would rest often on a stone seat under a fir by the little house where he lived and which they called Le Petit Trianon. Madame Lavallière had made it a term of the handing over of the château that her former employees should be housed there. That, at any rate, was the usual place where he sat and smoked and looked at the flowers he had once tended.

We went out again into the sunlight. The birds sang; it was very still and peaceful and we threaded our way along gravelled paths between the flowerbeds where tulips and roses created a blaze of colour. We found him easily enough, as we had been told, on a stone seat in the shade of the spreading branches of a tall fir. He was wearing a faded blue cap and a grey smock affair which looked about as old as himself. A stick was beside him and an ancient curved pipe between his lips.

'Tell him,' I said to Jo, 'that we are relatives of madame who have lost touch with her and we heard of her château. Ask him if he knows whether she is still alive and if so where she now lives.'

She managed it very well but did not seem at first to have much success. He looked at us suspiciously out of grey eyes filmed with age. Then he coughed, hawked, looked at us again, looked away and shook his head slowly. There was a pause and then, all at once, he turned back and stared at Jo. Bending forward, he reached out a frail, old, liver-spotted hand to touch her arm. Drawing her towards him he peered up into her face. 'You are young,' he said. 'And very beautiful. You look so sad you remind me of her. Sadness takes the light from beauty. You will bring her no harm. I feel it here—' He touched his head. 'I will tell you of her.'

'*Merci*,' Jo said quietly.

'She went away and she came back,' he said. 'The first time . . .' He paused, thinking, his mind retracing the years. 'When the war was ending and after it, those were the bad days, months, years, accusations, jealousies, it was a time for the paying off of old scores. She was accused by some, she was bitter. She left, taking the boy with her.'

'Boy?' I said. 'What boy? Ask him, Jo.'

'Who was he?' Jo said but I doubt if he heard her. He was back in the past and his wits were wandering.

'I was only a gardener,' he said. 'She was denounced by the communists. She was saved from death by the remnants of the Resistance who came down from the hills. They knew who had served them and served them well. They and the Americans who came then, they protected her, but she wouldn't stay. She escaped to America. But the boy, they would have shot him but for her and the Americans. She hid him, where no one knows. And then she took him with her to America.'

'The boy,' Jo said again, softly, pleadingly, 'what was his name?'

Again he appeared to take no notice of her. 'She came back,' he said. 'These hills, they lay their hands on people's hearts and they must return to them. But those dark days are not all forgotten. There are still some who live in fear. Come, I shall show you . . .'

Taking his stick he clambered to his feet, his old bones creaking. Slowly, leaning on the stick, he led the way to a turreted gazebo on the terrace behind him. Curving stone steps gave access to its interior, one side of which save for a breast-high parapet was open to the sky. It afforded a view across the countryside of meadow and forest to the high dramatic mountains in the distance where cloud wreathed their high peaks. At the top of the steps he paused for breath, leaning on his stick. Then he moved to the parapet. 'Look,' he said. 'Look.' He raised his stick to his shoulder as if he were aiming a gun. Behind him I looked along it and then I saw it.

The high clouds parted for an instant, and there it was, visible in a cleft between the peaks, a grim forbidding fortress, a thing of towers and cupolas, of battlements and embrasures, dark against the vivid blue of the sky. 'The Fort du Martigny,' he said. 'It holds its secrets still.'

There was a stone bench running round the back of the gazebo opposite the parapet. As if exhausted by his efforts, he moved over to it and sat heavily down, his stick between his knees, his chin resting on it.

'Where is she now, Madame Lavallière?' Jo asked him softly.

'In the village of Lurdos,' he said surprisingly quickly. She sends me parcels, *tabac*—'

'Will she speak to us?'

'I do not know. That you must find for yourselves. She lives in seclusion seeing few, I'm told. She keeps her secrets too.'

'And the boy?' I said.

'He remained in America. Should he return there are several still here who would kill him.'

'Who was he? What did he do?' Jo asked.

'He was a foundling. She took him in. He had no name save what she gave him. He was the messenger. He betrayed them and her. She forgave, others do not. What name he has now or if he lives I know not, but if he is alive I hope he remembers and I hope he lives in hell.' He leant forward and spat on the floor at our feet.

'He seems remarkably well informed,' I said to Jo.

As if he heard me and understood he raised his old eyes to mine. 'I was a communist, m'sieu,' he said.

To reach Lurdos we had to cross another mountain chain, going by the Col de Blaque which turned and twisted its lonely way through the hills before descending on to a rolling, downland plain.

'So it was Amory,' Jo said as we went.

'It must have been,' I said. 'Mr Clean, how are you now?

But that's the hold Francis Aloysius has over him, I'll bet, however he got it.'

'But he's so young, I can't imagine him being in the war.'

'That's just it, that's what misled us. Maybe he did have a face lift like Jack Manley said. Anyway, we don't know the details and we don't know for certain and there's only one person who can tell us.'

'Madame Lavallière?'

'That's right, and even she may not know what's behind it all. Here we are.'

It was a tiny mediæval village tucked into a fold in the downs, its stone-built houses crowding together as if in protection. The first person we met on entering it was the curé, black-hatted and coated, meandering along, head down, reading his missal. 'Ask him where she lives, he's sure to know,' I said.

Whether we had disturbed him at his office or he was reluctant to divulge her whereabouts I don't know, but he hesitated a bit until, on being told we were relatives, he gave us instructions. The house, he said, was at the far end of the village, on the left, with blue windows.

It was small and built of the same sort of stone as the rest, with a trim garden in front and a flagged path leading to the door. A bell and a knocker were set into an upper panel but no one answered either. After waiting and trying again I pushed on the door. It was securely locked. No one was at home, or if they were, they were paying no heed to visitors. I don't quite know why but there was a sort of stillness around, a lack of life I didn't like. A feeling of apprehension mounted inside me. 'Let's try the back,' I said.

Another flagged pathway brought us round the end of the house to the rear door. This had a latch and a keyhole underneath. I tried the latch and it opened. Pushing it wide enough to enter I looked around it and stepped inside. Jo followed me into a trim kitchen. On a deal table beside the cooker a meal had been set but it had not been eaten. Bread and cheese, a plate of cold meat and a flask of wine were laid out, but the meat and the cheese had hardened and the bread was stale.

We looked at each other. There was no sound at all in the house. Very gently I called 'Hallo' and then, 'Anyone there?' No answer came. 'We'll have to look around,' I said. 'Something has happened, I can feel it in my bones.'

The two front rooms on either side of a narrow hall were furnished as a study and a sitting-room. Nothing had been disturbed here. There was a telephone on a bureau in the study with a pad beside it but the pad was blank and held no message. Upstairs was a room at the front, obviously hers with a bed made up; dresses hung in a built-in cupboard and toilet accessories were on the dressing-table. All was neat and undisturbed, as was a tidy adjoining bathroom and a second bedroom with twin beds.

'All very clean and tidy,' I said. 'And yet something's wrong, I'm sure of it. Why did she leave her meal untouched and the back door on the latch? I reckon it was because she left in a tremendous hurry. But why?' I went to the window and looked out. As I stood there, opposite us, in another similar house, I saw a curtain twitch and a face being hastily withdrawn. 'Don't look now,' I said to Jo. 'But we are observed. Someone across the way is taking an interest in us. We'll go slowly to the car, stand together as if we were discussing what to do next. I fancy she's curious, that lady opposite, and she'll come again.'

She did. Scarcely had we reached the car when the curtain opposite was once more cautiously drawn back and a face peered out. 'We'll see what she has to say for herself,' I said. 'She knows something or she wouldn't be so interested.'

I strode up the little path identical with that which we

had just left and banged on the door. It opened almost immediately and I found myself staring into an old face drawn and lined and a pair of deepset, dark eyes alive with curiosity and, yes, malice. While I was grappling with my French Jo took over yet again. We were relatives of Madame Lavallière, she said and were anxious to find her. We had news for her but she seemed to have gone away.

'Relatives?' croaked the old witch—for that was what she looked like and the stick in her hand could well have doubled for a broomstick. 'I never heard of any. She sees no one, that one. She lives to herself, no one comes, no one goes—now she has gone, in a hurry and has not returned.'

'Gone?' Jo echoed. 'When?'

'Yesterday,' came the answer. 'I heard a telephone ring there and then she came rushing out to her little car and off with her—furiously. It's strange. In all the years she has never gone away before.'

'You can't help us, then,' Jo said. 'When is she likely to return?'

'Return?' There came a cackle of ancient laughter. 'Never, perhaps. Maybe it's the past. She lives in the past, that one. The past,' she said again. 'She is so proud. What has she to be proud of? Her past, what was it—maybe you are of it too—' Suddenly, looking at us as if she saw us for the first time, she took a step backwards and slammed the door in our faces.

There was nothing further to be gained here. We returned to the car.

'Where can she have gone?' Jo said.

'There was a threat, that telephone call, I'll bet,' I said. 'It summoned her away.'

'But how can we find her?'

'There's only one course left to us now,' I said. 'Only one place that we know of and that's where we must go.'

'Stop talking in riddles, Charles. Where?'

'The place Aristide said still holds its secrets,' I said. 'The Fort du Marigny. Where's the map?'

Together we leant over it. 'There it is,' I said, pointing, 'and it doesn't look all that far away.'

She stared out through the windscreen. 'I hate the thought of that place,' she said. 'It gives me the shivers. Charles, look, why don't we pack all this in, and just cut and run?'

'Where to?' I said sombrely. 'I only wish we could. Don't deceive yourself. They'll be after us wherever we are. Our only hope is to keep in front of them, to find out what they're up to before they find us.'

'I suppose so,' she said doubtfully.

'Look what they've done already,' I said. 'They've killed the Colonel and tried to kill me. They'd have hi-jacked you if we hadn't slipped the net. I did think of pushing you off somewhere safe—but where?'

'Oh no,' she said. 'We're in this together. I'm being faint-hearted, aren't I? Not a bit like tough old Jo, the bully of the form, the horse-coping, hockey-sticks girl you thought me when we were growing up.'

'I never thought that.'

'You did, you know. Actually I've just thought of something the Colonel used to say he'd repeat to himself when things were bad. It's a quotation for you, Mr Brains, I hope I've got it right. Here it is: "Go fetch me down my gun, I ain't much hand at fightin' but I'll die before I run."'

'That's my girl. Let's along, then.' I started the car and as we moved off I raised my eyes to the window above us. As I thought, the curtains parted once more and those bright malicious eyes stared down at us, openly this time. I wondered if she knew more than she had said.

We found the main road to Spain and, leaving it, entered the far, frowning mountains. A great gorge embraced us with high cliffs rearing up on either side. Rounding a corner, we saw a battered sign pointing: FORT DU MARIGNY.

To our left a narrow bridge crossed a torrent far below and from it a rutted roadway led upwards. It climbed in a series of zigzags, corkscrews and hairpins through which our little car bustled and bounced until we came to a place where the winter rains pouring down had swept away the surface and the retaining wall, leaving a gaping chasm and only a narrow pathway for passing onwards and upwards. Beside it was a clearing in the undergrowth into which I ran the car. Then, skirting the chasm, we continued on foot.

We were now very high, so much so that my ears began to blurp. A few more twists and a tunnel through solid rock brought us to an open space and there, on its farther side, was the fort. It was a huge and monstrous edifice built on all levels into the face of the mountain and must have covered acres in extent. There were tiers of buildings with barred windows facing the gorge, behind them were towers and turrets with frowning empty gun emplacements dotted about, while fitted in here and there as it were, were what looked like modern buildings for the staff.

Facing us was a bridge over a ravine which seemed to go down for ever. At the far end of this was a massive steel double door, one half of which was slightly ajar. Somewhere far below us cars slid along the road we had left but no sound of their passing reached us. Despite the sun and the blue skies, it was cold up here and those vast empty buildings seemed to add to the loneliness and the chill. There was, too, an air of brooding evil about the place which one could almost feel. The Gestapo had left their legacy of darkness behind them; no screams could have been heard from here.

We crossed the bridge and I pushed at the steel door. It opened slowly, creaking noisily as it did so, the sound echoing eerily in the stillness. Entering, we found ourselves in a short passage which led to what appeared to be a small parade ground. To our right was what must have been a guardroom. Deserted now, its windows broken, a flight of steps led down to unknown cavernous depths. In front of us, across the parade ground, was one of the more modern buildings. I led the way towards it.

The door was open and we went in. As we did so a voice spoke from the dark interior. 'Shut the door behind you and don't move,' it said.

As my eyes accustomed themselves to the darkness I made out a figure sitting in a chair facing us. In his hand was a stubby hand-gun pointing at us and the hand that held it belonged to Francis Aloysius O'Shaughnessy.

CHAPTER 14

I knew enough about guns now to recognize a snub-nosed Smith and Wesson when I saw one and I knew enough about people to realize that he knew how to use it and would have little hesitation in doing so. Always before I had felt that basically he was a faintly ludicrous figure, a showman and little else and not to be taken seriously. I didn't now. He looked cold and hard and determined. His little eyes sunk deep into their sockets stared at us balefully and unblinkingly. The gun in his hand didn't waver an inch.

Feeling instinctively that we had to make him talk and keep talking, I sought for some way of doing just that. As it happened, Jo forestalled me. 'Why did you kill my father?' she said. 'You did, didn't you?'

'He recognized Amory,' he said. 'And he wouldn't tell us how much he knew—or guessed. He had to die just as you, who have so stupidly interfered, will have to die.' As he said that his eyes blazed with a sort of fanaticism. It was gone almost as soon as it came but I had caught it and suddenly I had a glimpse of what might be behind it all.

'Just how do you propose to do that?' I said. 'There's a law in this country, after all.' I was more than ever now determined to keep him talking to learn more and to try to probe for some weakness in him. It was our only chance.

'This place is full of traps for the unwary,' he answered me. 'You two young fools will have been exploring—a rock fall, a blunder into space, loose masonry on a battlement, a missing staircase—few come here and those that do don't penetrate far. It will be weeks, months, years before you are found—if ever.'

'I don't think you'll find it quite as easy as that,' I said. 'Before I left I gave a record of what I was doing and where I was going. If I don't return a search will be made.'

He looked at me contemptuously. 'You needn't think I'll take any notice of that,' he said. 'It's the oldest trick in the game. Who did you leave this so-called record with? That useless solicitor, I suppose. What can he do? Nothing.'

Then I had my brainwave. 'Oh no,' I said. 'It's not the solicitor and I'm not fooling. Far from it. It's my friend from the SAS. I've named you and told him if I didn't come back he was to go looking for you. You're a fairly flamboyant figure. I don't imagine he'll have much trouble finding you. You know the SAS. They don't ask many questions. He and his chums will catch up with you all right and I don't much envy you when they do.'

That got to him. If there's one thing calculated to send shivers down the spines of his sort it's a mention of the SAS. He blinked, and then, 'Don't fool with me,' he said in a sort of snarl.

'I'm not,' I said. 'And you know I'm not. He'll get through to you and get you, never fear.'

He hesitated. I could almost read his thoughts as he allowed what I had said to sink in. 'You're bluffing,' he said.

'If I am it's going to cost you to call me, isn't it?' I said.

Silence fell between us then for a minute or two. Suddenly, without taking his eyes off us, he shouted, 'Dinny!' And again, 'Dinny, damn you, here!'

There was the patter of feet outside, the door opened and the diminutive figure of Dinny Malone whom I had last seen at the Craddockstown Stud, entered.

'I might have known you'd be mixed up in this somewhere, Dinny,' Jo said, looking at him. 'You always were a shitty little man.'

'Tie 'em up,' commanded O'Shaughnessy. 'Their hands behind their backs.'

Dinny went out, returning in a few minutes with two lengths of nylon cord. With these he proceeded to bind our hands, leaving our feet free.

'All right. Now—outside.' O'Shaughnessy gestured towards us with the gun.

We came again into the sunlight of the parade ground and stood there for a moment. I looked at Jo and she looked at me. We both knew that he had made up his mind one way or another and it wasn't a nice feeling to think that we might be on our way to execution.

'In there,' he said, pointing to an archway in a far corner. 'You lead on, Dinny.'

In a little procession we made our way though the archway and down a long, sloping passage. At its foot we turned into another passage. Some way along this, at O'Shaughnessy's shouted order, we stopped beside an iron door. 'Open it,' he said to Dinny. When the bolts had been pulled, 'Inside,' he said to me, gesturing again with the gun.

It was a small, cell-like place. There was a barred window in the wall opposite, a rusty iron bedstead and a battered-looking chair. The door clanged shut behind us, we heard the bolts being shot and we were alone. Jo sat down on the bed whose ancient springs creaked and groaned. 'Well, at least we're alive,' she said.

'In a sort of photofinish,' I said. 'It was the mention of the SAS that swung it. Those chaps, they're shit-scared of the SAS and anything to do with them.'

'Did you leave a message? Is that true?'

'Most of it. I told Denzil Colton to come looking for me if I didn't turn up. And I named Francis Aloysius. He's in for a nasty few minutes if we don't come back and I reckon he knows it.'

'What will he do?'

'That's the question which is bothering him just about now, I imagine.'

'So what do we do?'

'Try to get out of these bonds for starters. We've got a breathing space anyway.'

'And the fat lady hasn't started to sing yet.'

'Maybe she's lost her voice. You never know.'

'And I'll tell you something. Dinny didn't tie me up all that tight.'

'What? After what you called him?'

'He always had good hands and he never liked knocking fillies about however badly they behaved. I remember him saying that once.'

'It didn't extend to me. He's trussed me tight enough. But let's see if I can get any purchase on yours if we stand back to back.'

She came over. 'But what can we do if we do get free?' she said.

'One jump at a time,' I said. 'We'll do this first.'

He had bound my arms above the wrists allowing my hands some freedom of movement. Feeling the cords that bound her, I found they were indeed slacker than mine. If I could find the knot and could loosen it, it was probable she could slide her hands free. But I was groping blind. It took a good few minutes before I got to the knot and even then I didn't know if I could get enough purchase to manage to shift it. Feeling along the cords, I tried to make out its shape.

'Any luck?' she said.

'Not much. This is where one wishes one was a Boy Scout.'

'No one would mistake you for one of those, Charles.'

Desperately I tried to form a picture in my mind of the way in which he would have tied the cords. 'Can you move your wrists at all?' I asked her.

'Yes, a bit.'

'Do it now, will you?'

She wriggled them and the cord moved ever so slightly. Then, following it, I found the knot. It was on the outside, which was a help. In addition there was a loose end. Gently I followed it back to the body of the knot. There I could feel where it intersected with the other cords. And then came the crunch. If I did the wrong thing I would tighten the bond instead of loosening it. Feeling further, I found that thanks to Dinny's kindness with fillies or his reluctance to bruise female flesh, the knot was just that much looser than it might have been. I got a finger under it and began to work at the join. At first nothing happened. Then, ever so slightly, it moved. My nail broke but that didn't matter, for whatever I was doing was accomplishing something. It slackened and I could feel the gap in the cords widening. Now came another crunch—should I push or pull? Push I reckoned. I did, it gave and slowly I eased it through the gap. It came free and then I had two loose cords in my hands. Pulling them towards me, I felt the whole thing slacken. 'Move your wrists slightly,' I said. 'Are they freer?'

'Yes, I can move them up and down.'

'Can you squeeze your hands through?'

I awaited her reply while I felt the movement in her wrists. She struggled and then: 'No,' she said. 'It just won't go.'

'OK. Hold on. I'll see if I can loosen them a bit more.'

It wasn't as difficult as I expected. Suddenly the cords fell away and she was free. That was one of us. 'Can you do the same for me?' I said.

She examined my wrists. 'Gosh,' she said. 'He's done you all right. It's going to be a job, but I'll try.'

'Don't,' I said then. 'See that window? If you stand on the bed you can reach it. Take off a shoe and smash it. A sliver of broken glass will cut the cords.'

She climbed on to the bed, the glass broke and in a minute or two she was back with a razor-sharp piece in her hand. It sliced through the cords and both of us were free.

'The next thing to do is to get out of here,' I said. 'I don't think that window is going to be much help.'

Getting on the bed, I stood on it and looked out. All that did for me was to command a view of the mountains opposite. The bars were solid and firmly embedded and so far as I could see there was a sheer drop beneath us.

When I got down again I looked around for a weapon. Someone had to come for us sooner or later and if it was only Dinny or O'Shaughnessy we might have a chance of surprising them. I went over to the chair. It had been strongly enough made but it was riddled with worm and seemed about to fall apart. Taking hold of one of its legs, I pulled and it came away in my hand. It wasn't much but it would have to do. Holding it, I went over and put my ear to the door. There was silence outside for a bit and then I heard it. Footsteps were coming down the passage. We had only just freed ourselves in time.

'Stand opposite the door,' I hissed at Jo. 'When it opens, scream. It may distract their attention enough to allow me to get a wallop at them. I'll be beside the door.'

I took up my position. The footsteps came closer and then there was the sound of bolts being drawn back.

The door opened slowly.

I glanced at Jo as it swung ajar. Her mouth opened but the scream froze on her lips. She stared at the doorway and a hand crept up to her mouth. I turned back and raised the chair-leg. It, too, was halted in mid-air. A tall, elegant, elderly woman stood on the threshold. The lines on her face which age had written there could not conceal the bone structure beneath them. She must have been very beautiful once. I knew immediately who she was.

CHAPTER 15

We stared at each other in silence for a few moments, my arm still poised. Then I lowered it. 'Madame Lavallière?' I said.

'You are correct,' she said with the briefest of smiles. 'And you are M'sieu Hampton and Mam'selle Manners. Come, quickly.'

She swung the door to behind us and shot the bolts. We followed her through endless dank, stone-flagged passages until at length we came to a flight of steps leading to an oaken, iron-studded door set in an archway. Taking a bunch of keys from a pocket, she opened this and beckoned us to follow. Once inside, I gasped. It was a huge room. A long mahogany table ran almost its entire length flanked on either side by ranks of ornately carved chairs. At the far end was a cavernous stone fireplace and above it hung a portrait of Hitler in his brown shirt and Sam Browne glowering down at us. The whole place was thick with dust which lay like a film along the table. She saw my astonishment and turned to me. 'This was the officers' mess when the Germans occupied the place,' she said. 'I was here then. I know every inch of the fort for I had the run of it—once. There was a plan long ago just after the war to open it all as a museum piece, a tourist attraction, but it came to nothing and the fort was left as it was, discarded and forgotten save by those with long memories.'

'Why are you here now, madame?' I said. 'And why have you freed us?'

'I am here because they fooled me,' she said. 'They told me that Amory Brayne, my ward, was here and in trouble and asking for me. It was a trap to entice you, as I soon found out. They little knew that I had keys to every door, that I knew far more than they did of the fort and its ramifications, its hiding places and escape routes. Oh yes, escape routes. At the end of the war when they knew it was lost the Boche made ready to leave and provided themselves with ways of doing it unobserved.'

'Where is Francis Aloysius now?' Jo asked her.

'Do not be afraid,' she said. 'Something one of you said frightened him. He is sitting with a bottle of whisky thinking what he should do next with you—and himself.'

'But what will he do to you when he discovers you have freed us?' Jo asked her.

'Nothing, child,' she said. 'I am not afraid of him. Besides, he thinks I am securely locked up.'

Suddenly she was seized by a paroxysm of coughing which racked her whole body. I pulled back a chair and she slumped into it, bent over, helpless, torn by dreadful coughs which told of only one thing. At length they passed. Gasping for breath, steadying herself with her hands on the table, she sat up. 'As you can see,' she said, 'I am dying. I have nothing to lose except my life and that is lost already.'

I waited for the effects of the spasm to pass, then I said to her as she groped for a handkerchief and passed it over her lips: 'What do you know of O'Shaughnessy? What is his secret which he is so desperately trying to hide that he will kill for it? He has threatened, no tried, to kill us and he killed Jo's father, Colonel Manners.'

She looked hard at Jo. 'I should have guessed,' she said. 'There is the resemblance but after all these years memory fades. So you are Tomo's girl. Tomo, that's what we called your father. He was so spirited, so spry, so gay, but that's a word I must not use now, must I? I remember him so well though. Dear Tomo—' For a moment her old eyes lit up and I saw something of what she must have been like in those days of the Resistance—young, fiery, vibrant. Then the flicker died and she was old again with the flame of life fading within her. 'I will help you, I promise,' she said. 'But first, what do you know of me and of Amory?'

I told her what we had learnt. 'I have to say this,' I finished. 'It was Amory Brayne or whatever name he went by then, wasn't it, who betrayed the plan to rescue Renard?'

'He was only a boy,' she said defensively. 'He was the messenger. He ran errands for the Boche and kept his ears open and brought us such information as he could. They should never have used him to smuggle their plan to Renard I told them so. I begged them not to. So did Tomo. He backed me up but it was no use. The trouble was, some in the Resistance did not trust me and others even were suspicious of the Englishman. No one trusted another in those terrible days. Brother betrayed brother and sometimes sister betrayed them both. You children are too young to know anything of that awful time. Yes, he told them. They suspected him all along and they tricked or tortured him into telling. I saved him from the vengeance the maquisarde would have wreaked on him when the Boche threw him out labelled a traitor. It was difficult but I did it. I took him to America. I had friends in high places as well as low.' Then she was seized by another bout of coughing.

'And O'Shaughnessy?' I said when it had passed. 'How did he find out?'

'I shall tell you. Amory, as I'm sure you know for most people do, became a brilliant analytical chemist. He made money, a lot of money. When he was young and with us we had horses at the château, for my husband used to breed one or two to race at Pau. Amory fell in love with horses and that, Mr Hampton, as you must also know, is a love, perhaps the only one, which never dies. Using the money he made, he determined to go into racing in America. It was then that he was introduced to O'Shaughnessy. Amory, I must tell you, is not a strong character. Always he must have someone to lean on. For years I supplied that. He kept nothing from me—'

'And then,' I said. 'O'Shaughnessy came—'

'Yes. Amory conceived great admiration for him for the way he handled his racing affairs so successfully. They became friends as well as business associates, in fact O'Shaughnessy soon became his confidant. It was inevitable he would come to realize there was a secret hidden in Amory's past. He is a man who will never accept anyone or anything at face value. Always he has to probe for a weakness which he can exploit. Already he knew of the formula Amory had sold to the conglomerates, indeed there was no real secret about it.'

'What was—' I started to say but she waved me to silence.

'He questioned him about that past, oh so cleverly, over the weeks, months, dropping a hint here and a word there until he began little by little to piece the story together. Remember Amory liked and trusted him at that time and he allowed his guard, isn't that what you say, to slip a little. It was through horses that they had come together and Amory told him something of his love of them having been engendered by his youth at the château. That gave O'Shaughnessy his opening. He knew of me through Amory and we had met and I hated him on sight, the *canaille*. He tried to sound me out on the subject of Amory's past and I sent him away with as you would say a flea in his ear. But he stops at nothing, that one. He travelled here to find out more—and he found it. He had money and there were those who talked. There are always those, as you too have found. He returned to the States with something he could hold over Amory.'

'Camilla found a card from the fort marked with a cross,' I said.

'He kept it, did he? He told me of it. That was the start, sent from here to frighten him. Amory has grown away from me since all this has happened and O'Shaughnessy has come into his life, but we were still very close at that time though even then he kept me apart from Camilla, afraid, I suppose, that she might learn something of his origins from me. I knew something terrible had happened to him that was tearing him apart and I confronted him. I knew he would talk, for I was still a shoulder to weep upon. He told me all that O'Shaughnessy was doing to him, that he had found his secret and was blackmailing him.'

'It's a long time ago,' I said. 'I wonder how much exposure would matter now.'

'He came to America under a false passport,' she said, 'and has lived under a false name. I was responsible for that. I wanted to bury forever what had happened so that he could start anew. But if all this came out he could lose his citizenship. Remember that. And Amory is a sensitive man. He is now prominent in racing. Even at best think of the stigma and think, too, of the contracts he has signed, the money he has made—'

'Is it just money that O'Shaughnessy wants?' I said. 'Is he bleeding him dry or is it something else?'

'It is other than money, though money is at the back of it, which he wants for his own ends.'

'What is it, then,' I said, 'that Amory had which O'Shaughnessy wanted so badly that he was prepared to blackmail for it?'

'It was the formula,' she said. 'Amory had found a formula for ensuring and perfecting if you like sexual prepotency in males. It was far from being just a nostrum or aphrodisiac, it was a fertility drug and it worked. Going further, he found or was about to find an addition whereby the sex of the unborn child could be determined at source. The conglomerate paid him an enormous sum so that they had the sole rights of marketing. Unfortunately they found that its side-effects made men savage; they could not use it commercially and they killed it. I was glad enough. It was tampering with nature. I hated it and I told him so.'

'Did he tell you what O'Shaughnessy wanted it for?' I said, though by now I knew.

'Not in so many words. He was affronted by my criticisms. But I know from what he did let drop. It was for the purposes of the stud—horse-breeding. He made him work to use it to that end. How I hated it all. I do not know if he was successful.'

'He was,' I said. 'In one instance at least it has turned a useless stallion into a prepotent one. What with AI and all these advances, it was bound to come sooner or later but Amory got in first.'

'I only wish he hadn't. Look what has come of it. A wedge was driven between us. He drifted apart from me. I seldom hear from him now. I said from the start that no good would come of it and I was right—ourselves separated, Tomo killed, poor Tomo, and you two in danger of your lives. And now, my children, we have spent too much time in talking. You must go.' Once more she led the way along endless passages and flights of steps, through deserted rooms and past rows of what it seemed were once partitioned offices until at last we came to a door set in a blank wall. 'This is where the break-in was that fatal night,' she said. 'Then they scaled the cliff face, now there is a platform and steps, another relic of the plans for tourism. *Son et lumière* was what was proposed; it was as well they abandoned it. You will find the steps, they will take you to a path cut in the cliff which leads to the front of the fort. But take care, the path is narrow and the steps are old.'

Thankfully a moon had come up so we could more or less see our way, though the prospect to say the least of it looked uninviting. The handrail on the steps was broken in places and there were unmentionable depths below. She sensed my hesitation. 'There is no other way,' she said. 'I daren't take you to the main part of the fort in case he is there and searching. Go now and *bonne chance, mes enfants*.'

'But you, madame,' I said. 'Cannot you come with us?'

'No,' she said. 'I shall stay. I want to see that *canaille* suffer and rage at your going. But should you see Amory tell him that my memories of him are all fond. Now—GO!'

It was a command. I turned as we reached the top step from the platform and the last I saw of her she was standing by the open door, tall, imperious and sad. She raised a hand and then the door closed behind her.

We crept down the steps feeling our way. They were crumbling in places and I dared not look out over the ravine beneath us. At their end they gave on to the narrow path she had mentioned. Cut into the solid rock, it had no handrail at all. At least the shadows cast by the fort hid something of the enormity of the sheer drop on our outside. Once Jo slipped and it was only my sudden grasp of her arm that saved her. Altogether it was a breathtaking business. Everything seemed quiet in the fort as it loomed above us. And so after ten minutes of perilous passage we came into the glacis beside the bridge leading to the entry, where another flight of steps brought us to the carriageway and freedom.

The car was where we had left it. I rolled her down the steep approach road and round the bends with the engine off and the moon giving us light enough so as not to betray our going with the headlights. Then I drove to Pau. We caught the early plane to Paris and despite the complexities of Charles de Gaulle and scrabbling for seats, twenty-four hours later saw us breakfasting at the flat.

CHAPTER 16

In a way it had all seemed unreal as we sat over coffee and toast next morning but of course it wasn't: it was very real indeed and nothing had gone from the peril in which we stood, of that I was sure since Francis Aloysius was not the man to give up easily. We happened to be a jump in front of him now and I reckoned we'd better try to keep it that way. My thoughts were running on how to do just that and Jo's, it seemed, were much the same. 'What now?' she said as she poured coffee.

'The Irish Derby is tomorrow,' I said. 'That may have slipped your memory. It nearly did mine.'

'It had, as a matter of fact. I'd other things on my mind as you may have noticed. Why?'

'I'm going to have a word, or more than a word with Amory Brayne.'

'Amory? Hasn't he suffered enough!'

'Maybe, but he holds the key. They're up to something and that colt Midsummer Day is only part of it. I don't quite know what it is, though I've an idea. You heard what Louise Lavallière said about the formula. I think they've been experimenting with that sire of his, Hunter's Moon. If I'm right, Amory is at the heart of it. That's what Francis Aloysius has been blackmailing him for. That's why I want to get to him and quickly. It's obvious now. They gave Hunter's Moon the dosage and he got Midsummer Day and somehow the genes jumped right for them and he's avoided the side-effects. That can happen. But the point is there's more behind it all. Even Francis Aloysius wouldn't go to the lengths of killing just for the money involved. He's up to something else and Amory is only part of it.'

'Look, Charles, let's be clear about this. I like Amory. I don't give a tinker's curse what he did before I was born. It's all ancient history anyway. He's been a good friend to me. It's Francis Aloysius we want to stop, though how we can do it I don't know. I'll not have any hand, act or part in harassing Amory any more.'

'You're wrong,' I said. 'It's only through him we can find the truth and get at Francis Aloysius.'

'Well, you do it by yourself, then. I'm not coming with you to the Irish Derby. That's your idea, isn't it—to confront him there somehow? Go ahead, then, but without me. And I hope his colt wins, what's more.'

'That's something I want to see.'

'By yourself, then, Charles.'

'Somehow, somewhere he fits into the picture, and knows it too.' I said, 'And I aim to make him talk. Which reminds me I must ring Denzil and tell him we're back in one piece more or less.'

He answered the phone and I told him there was no need for the 7th Cavalry to come galloping to the rescue and I'd give him the whole story later on. 'In the meantime,' I added, 'I want some information if you can give it to me. Is Midsummer Day from the first crop by Hunter's Moon since they brought him back?'

'That's right. And it's a funny thing, they didn't give him any outside mares. I don't know what happened to the others. And he only got a few mares in foal when he was in

Japan. He was damn near infertile. That's why they got him so cheap.'

'Do you know if there were any other bargain basement sires they bought there or anywhere?'

'Odd you should ask that. I was having a drink with Jim Oldton of the *Daily World* the other day. He's about ninety, as you probably know, but he's as clear as a bell and he has always been a breeding pundit and knows the stud books backwards. There's been a good bit of talk about Midsummer Day, as you can imagine. He said they had Herodotus, you may remember him, he won the King George VI in a bad year and turned out a complete failure at stud. He was sold to the Argentine and they bought him back, but he turned out so savage they could hardly get him to cover a mare. He was put down in the end. Jim said he'd heard Hunter's Moon was on the savage side too. He thought it all most peculiar.'

'So do I,' I said.

I told Jo of what Denzil had said. 'So you see it all looks more and more as if you were right when you said you thought there was something odd about Hunter's Moon that day at Craddockscourt.'

'What if I was, Charles? I'm still not going to do anything to damage Amory.'

Amory Brayne, I reflected, must have something going for him since that made three women of varying ages all prepared to go bat for him. Jo had her determined little chin out in the well-remembered way and once again I knew that that danger signal meant it was of no avail to try arguing with her.

'As you wish,' I said. 'And it's perhaps as well that I go this one alone. But what are we to do with you? You can't stay here. Francis Aloysius knows only too well where I live. He may be coming looking already.'

'I'll go to Aunt Jessica in Clapham. I'll be safe there.'

'I wish—' I said and then stopped. Words weren't going to help.

She saw my hesitation and her expression softened. She stretched out a hand and I took it. 'Dear Charles,' she said, 'I'm sorry. It's the way I'm made. We were all the same, the three of us, the Colonel, Mike and me, good friends and good haters. Once we've given affection we can't take it back. I couldn't come in on harassing Amory and anyway you'll do far better without me.'

That last might be true, I thought, but I hated leaving her. 'I only hope you'll be safe,' I said. 'Here is Denzil's number.' I tore a sheet from the pad beside the telephone and wrote it down. 'Ring him if you see any odd or suspicious characters hanging about. He'll come galloping to the rescue.'

'Like the 7th Cavalry,' she said.

'That's it. Now let's not stand upon the order of our going, as Mr Shakespeare said or something like it anyway, but go.'

Just to be on the safe side we left the flat by the rear entrance I had used before. A taxi took us to Clapham and after I dropped her I went on alone to Heathrow. We had been through so much together it seemed strange not to have her by my side. Everything, in fact, seemed empty without her. But I pushed those thoughts away and tried to concentrate on thinking how I was to get Amory alone and handle him when I did. I had a gut feeling now that whatever they were up to depended on Midsummer Day and surely Francis Aloysius would not want him to win without being present, unless of course he was chasing round France looking for us, which seemed unlikely.

The first obstacle I met was to find that admission to the Curragh Members' enclosure was by ticket only and I hadn't got one. In a way that suited me well enough. I could go to the lesser grandstand enclosure where my talent for fading into the background was better exercised away from the fashionable throng. There I could lurk unseen and wait and watch for an opportunity to collar Amory. Francis Aloysius was such a flamboyant figure and so anxious for the limelight that I was bound to spot him somewhere. But I didn't. He wasn't round the weighroom nor in the parade ring for any of the preliminary races. Even when the runners for the Derby came in he wasn't there either. In fact Amory was quite alone with his trainer, making idle conversation, I supposed, in the way one does in those tetchy moments before a big race.

I decided that this was the best place to tackle him. It was taking a chance, exposing myself to the public gaze as it were and that of Francis Aloysius if he happened to be about, but as of that moment I was in the business of taking chances. I walked boldly up to the man at the entrance to the parade ring. I have found before that if you present yourself to those guardians of the gate as if you had business inside they seldom question you, and it worked. He dropped the cord straightaway and I crossed the cropped grass to where Amory stood. His back was turned to me and I touched him on the arm. When he saw me it took a moment for recognition to sink in. Then he gave a little gasp. 'Mr Hampton,' he said. 'I thought you were abroad.'

'I was,' I said. 'I've been seeing an old friend of yours, Madame Lavallière.'

He took a step backward and his tongue ran across his lips gone suddenly dry. He had paled a bit, too. 'Louise,' he said. 'But how did you—'

'I have a message for you from her,' I said. 'It's private and urgent. I must see you and alone. You will realize I think the reason why we must be alone, Mr Brayne, if I may call you that.'

I wanted to rattle him and I succeeded. He got the

message all right and I thought he turned a shade paler. 'Very well,' he said. 'Come to my box after the last race.'

'Alone,' I said. 'Remember that. No Francis Aloysius. Where is he, by the way? I thought he'd be by your side.'

'He's been called away on urgent business,' he said. 'Now, if you'll excuse me—'

I had timed my entrance well. The jockeys had just come in. The diminutive figure of Paddy O'Day, the champion Irish jockey, approached us and touched his cap with his whip. What went on between the connections of Midsummer Day and what instructions were given was none of my business. I drifted away but since I was in the ring I took the opportunity of studying the runners. A look at the betting told me that Midsummer Day was favourite at 2–1. An English colt, Golightly, who had run fourth at Epsom was next at 5–1 and the French challenger, L'Epée, was on the same mark. The rest, I thought, from a field of eight, were mostly no-hopers.

They were beginning to form up preparatory to going out so I hurried away to get a place on the packed stands. In the parade Midsummer Day was quiet and composed and showing no signs of temperament.

'He'll win nothing,' the man beside me said. 'The Frenchman'll win this. That Bennerton who trains for Brayne, he couldn't train one to win an argument.' Racing talk, I said to myself, it's the same the whole world over, and in any event I didn't think my neighbour was right. Midsummer Day looked to me—though I never regarded myself as anything of a judge—hard and fit and trained to the minute. Midsummer Day continued to behave like a gentleman in the long trip across the Curragh to the start, nor did he give any trouble entering the stalls. In fact they all went in without incident and in a few minutes they were off. It was a clear day and I could pick out Amory's colours without any trouble. One of the outsiders was cutting out the work and Midsummer Day had settled nicely in the middle of the field. They were lost to view for a short space behind a rise in the ground and then emerged before the turn for home and the long, punishing, finishing straight.

The field were well bunched now. The Frenchman had moved up to the outsider and two others were racing on his left. They were really running for home by this time and the Frenchman had gone for his race. Midsummer Day still had a wall of horses in front of him. It looked to me like a very rough race as they converged on the leader and still Midsummer Day was boxed in. Suddenly an opening presented itself and O'Day drove his colt into it. Midsummer Day was game enough to take the chance and had the class and speed to get away with it. But they were inside the furlong pole and L'Epée had got first run.

Hard driven Midsummer Day was cutting down the distance stride by stride but would the winning post come too soon? There was a roar of cheering all around me. I sensed that L'Epée was tiring and Midsummer Day had every chance of catching him. Still up. On the rails he drew abreast and for an instant they raced side by side. So far as I could see there was plenty of room on the inside. But something happened. Whether L'Epée, tiring, left the straight course and rolled on Midsummer Day or whether Midsummer Day came away from the rail and interfered with L'Epée was to be a source of discussion for months afterwards. It's notoriously difficult to judge these things from the side, which was where I was, but what mattered was that Midsummer Day had got his head in front and kept it there to the post.

The result came over the loudspeakers. Midsummer Day had won. L'Epée second, the distance half a length and four lengths. This was immediately followed by the announcement of a stewards' inquiry. 'Hope they've got a good interpreter,' my loquacious neighbour said. 'I hear that

French jockey hasn't a word of English save "Oh sheet."'

I wandered off thinking about the inquiry. It was true Midsummer Day had come through a pretty narrow opening, but from what I had seen there was room and he hadn't touched anything. Then at the end of the race they had indeed come close but it seemed to be six of one and half a dozen of the other. But you never knew with stewards and their advisers. It could go either way and they would have the benefit of the head-on picture which I hadn't. In any event it suited my book. I wanted Brayne off balance and rattled so that I could shake him some more, and waiting for the result of the inquiry wouldn't do his nerves any good especially since they were already on the stretch before the race, if I was any judge.

The result of the inquiry was the hell of a long time coming. Maybe the language barrier of which my neighbour had spoken had something to do with it. It wasn't until another race had come and gone that we got it: the result stood, there was no alteration in the placings. So whatever schemes Francis Aloysius and Amory Brayne were hatching, if they depended on Midsummer Day winning the race they could carry on and what those schemes were I aimed shortly to find out.

After the last race I gave Brayne a little time to clear his box as there were bound to be a few celebrants, free-loaders and hangers-on still there. Then I made my way up to it. His was one of the new range of boxes at the far end of the grandstand.

He was quite alone, standing by the window looking out over the Curragh. A newly opened bottle of champagne was on the table with two glasses beside it. He turned at my entry and I noticed there were lines of strain round his mouth and eyes. 'Ah, Mr Hampton,' he said. 'You will take a glass of wine to drink to our success?'

'I'm not sure I will,' I said.

He stared at me blankly for a moment. 'You say you have news from Louise,' he said then, looking at me questioningly.

'She wishes you well,' I said. 'Which is more than I do.' Unlike the ladies, I wasn't disposed to be sympathetic to Amory Brayne. I had decided that from the outset I would lead trumps in an effort to rattle him into giving me the information I needed. 'You see,' I went on, 'I know you are not what you seem, Mr Amory Brayne. I know what you did all those years ago at the Fort du Marigny which led to the killing of your friends and the execution of Renard.'

All the colour drained from his face. He sat down heavily on one of the chairs. 'I've lived with it all my life,' he said. 'It's haunted me. Can't you understand?'

'But you have lived with it, haven't you?' I said. 'And lived very well too. That's what you've been afraid of, isn't it? Exposure. Losing all you've got. Possibly prosecution as a war criminal. That's why O'Shaughnessy was able to blackmail you.'

He tried to fend me off. 'Louise,' he said, 'how is she?'

'She's dying,' I said. 'But you haven't given her much thought recently, have you? O'Shaughnessy has got her too. Let's get back to him, shall we? What's he blackmailing you for?'

He spread his hands helplessly. 'Why should I tell you?' he said with a feeble attempt at defiance.

I looked at him and then, suddenly, I knew him for what he was, saw him stripped of the façade of charm and good fellowship. He was a hollow man even as he had been a weak, untrustworthy boy. He hadn't been tortured all those years ago, probably not even threatened. He'd only been frightened just as I was frightening him now. He had sought to keep in with what he thought to be the stronger side and he had talked. Afterwards he had lived with fear, fear of being found out, frightened all his life, and now it was my business to frighten him more.

'I'll tell you why you should talk and I'll tell you what I know,' I said. 'You found a formula for creating sexual prepotency in men and sold it to a conglomerate who killed it because of its side-effects. When O'Shaughnessy discovered what you had done in the war and traced you, he realized that if that formula could be adapted to horses he was on to a gold-mine. So he held the threat of exposure over you and set you to work. You got the sex angle right but there was still the side-effects to worry about and the first stallion you tried it on became so savage you had to shoot him. Are you with me so far and have I got it right?'

He nodded dumbly and I went on: 'But you went on working, didn't you, to cure those side-effects and when Hunter's Moon got Midsummer Day you thought you had it right in one colt anyway. I don't know what happened to the rest of the crop if there were any, and I don't care. The genes jumped right for Midsummer Day and when he won the Dewhurst you or O'Shaughnessy went nap on him. My guess is that O'Shaughnessy wanted the money for his own crazy or criminal purposes. He won the Guineas but O'Shaughnessy wanted more. He had to win the Irish Derby to get a bonanza syndication. He's done it, but in order to secure your secret he was prepared to kill. Why? What's he up to? What's behind it all? That's what I want to know and you're going to tell me. Remember I too can expose you now.'

Once more he ran his tongue over dry lips. He sighed helplessly, then suddenly the words came with a rush. 'I've had to live with this too,' he said. 'It's been another of my nightmares. I've longed to tell someone and couldn't. Since you know so much it's better you know the rest. Did you ever hear of the Organization for Irish Unity?'

'No,' I said.

'I didn't expect so. It's in its infancy. It's a breakaway from the IRA dedicated to bringing the armed struggle to the South as well as the North. O'Shaughnessy is its boss and moving spirit. In America, growing up, he was nurtured in the Republican spirit and tradition and he's eaten up with bitterness. He blames everything that happened to his family on what he calls the traitorous political junta of the South and their inheritors who have betrayed the ideals his father fought for. He has contacts everywhere—with Colonel Gaddafi, with the Basques, the Puerto Ricans and the Red Brigade, and his job gives him perfect cover. But up to now he was short of cash to finance his aims. He gambled on the syndication he had already arranged if Midsummer Day won the Derby here. Then he arranged a shipment of arms. It's arriving tonight, but he had to guarantee cash before he could take delivery. He did and it's come off. He was waiting word from me that the race was his so that he could go ahead and confirm he could pay.'

'I guessed it might be something like that,' I said, 'and the Colonel did too. That's why he spliced up that tape. Where is this delivery to take place?'

'A lonely beach in Kerry. That's where he is now.'

I saw it all then or thought I did. It was an ideal cover for O'Shaughnessy's plans, and the syndication and stud fees would be ideal vehicles for laundering money and no one would know of them save himself and Amory and possibly Dinny Malone, who would be well paid or frightened into keeping quiet. And the Colonel had guessed some of it, which was why he had to die. It was a pretty plot and I could imagine Francis Aloysius's fury when he thought we might be in possession of its details. 'And you've been helping him,' I said.

Once again came that gesture with his hands. 'What

could I do? He had me where he wanted me—over a barrel, isn't that what they say in this country?'

It crossed my mind to wonder just how genuine he was, why he was telling me all this so soon and so quickly. Then I dismissed the thought. He was a hollow man; resistance wasn't in him and he had come to the point where he had to unburden himself. That, as it happened, was my first mistake of the evening.

I didn't think I'd waste much more time on him. The sound of a helicopter landing came up to us and I saw him glance nervously towards the window, but I paid little attention to it as I was thinking out my next move. If I thought of it at all it was to imagine that some Arab was coming back to pick up a forgotten gold card or a case of Dom Perignon or a trophy he had at first thought he had not wanted for his overcrowded mantelpiece. That was my second mistake of the evening.

'Just where is this meeting taking place?' I said.

'If I tell you,' he answered, 'is there any way you can take him off my back?' Again I saw that slight look of shiftiness come into his eyes but I misread it.

'I can try,' I said. Now that I knew for certain, various options were running through my mind. I didn't get very far with them, for at that moment the door opened and Francis Aloysius came through it. In his hand was the same .38 Smith and Wesson I had seen before and as before it pointed directly at my stomach.

I looked at Amory. 'I should have guessed,' I said. 'When you rang to tell this hulking brute the result of the race you also told him I was here and had arranged to meet you. That's why you spilt the beans so quickly and so fully to me. You wanted to keep me talking until he arrived back in his chopper. Betrayal, that's your middle name, isn't it? You've let everyone down—Renard whom you got killed, and his friends, Colonel Manners among them, who nearly shared the same fate; Louise Lavallière to whom you owe everything and whom you left alone and forgotten in France. You say you have had to live with yourself. I don't envy you your company.'

He turned away from me to look out over the vast empty spaces of the Curragh. He spread his hands again in that gesture. 'What could I do?' he said almost piteously if one had any pity for him, which I hadn't.

I started to tell him so but I didn't get very far. Something hard hit me on the back of the head with a dull thud. I saw flashes; then I passed out.

CHAPTER 17

I never knew how they got me on to the helicopter. I suppose they half-dragged, half-carried me, letting on if anyone asked that I'd been celebrating their victory too well. Not that anyone was likely to ask many questions. It was *après racing* after all and people would be either concentrating on getting away from the crowded car parks or packing up and looking after their own affairs. Somewhere on the trip I came to briefly. I was dumped like a sack of coal in a rear seat, my hands were tied and I had a raging headache.

Gently opening my eyes, I saw that Francis Aloysius was piloting the thing and that we were alone. Amory presumably had been sent back to tidy up and generally mind the shop. My wits weren't working all that well, pain was shooting through my temples and the noise of the chopper made it worse. There was a hazy feeling, too, as if a curtain had been drawn between me and reality. The chopper gave a lurch, another shaft of pain shot through my head, the curtain came down and I went out again.

When I came to for the second time I was lying on a

camp bed in a small, bare room. My hands were still bound and I didn't know how long I'd been out for, but it must have been some considerable time since half-light was coming through the one window. I had a hideous taste in my mouth and guessed that they must have given me some sort of drug to keep me under. I felt half-doped and generally awful but the headache, at least, had gone.

I lay there for a bit thinking of my predicament and wondering what Francis Aloysius intended to do with me. It wasn't a pleasant prospect and there seemed little chance of evading it, whatever it was. My bonds, too, were secure. I tried straining against them and all that happened was to make them cut deeper into the skin. No way out there, so I lay on and tried to clear my clouded wits. After a bit I became aware of voices in the next room. Facing me was a communicating door. Hoisting myself off the bed, I made a cautious way towards it and put my ear to a panel. One of the voices belonged to Francis Aloysius and even if he tried, and he didn't seem to be trying very hard, he was unable to modify that bull-like roar. 'I'll give three flashes with the signal lamp,' he was saying. 'And you'll know it's all clear to come in. And by the way, I'll have a super-cargo for you.'

I couldn't hear the reply which was made in a much softer tone. Then there was the clink of glasses and the sound of chairs being pushed back. After that I heard a door shutting and then there was silence. I'd solved one problem anyway; it didn't take many guesses to learn who the super-cargo was—me—and it did little to revive my flagging spirits since a second guess would reveal that I wasn't intended to arrive at any destination. Another tug at my bonds didn't help either, nor did I know where we were save that I assumed it must be the place in the wilds of Kerry where the arms were to be landed after Francis Aloysius's signal with the lamp. A glance out of the window showed me a patchwork of little fields and faintly there came to me the smell of the sea and the thresh and splash of waves.

A period of complete silence followed, during which I went back to the bed and tried to control my nerves. Thank God, I thought, that at least Jo wasn't in it with me. It became steadily darker and so did my thoughts. A shower of rain dashed against the window.

At length the communicating door opened and Francis Aloysius came in. In his hand was a big signalling lamp and there was a bulge under his arm which I supposed concealed the Smith and Wesson. 'On your feet. Get up,' he barked at me. 'You're going on a long sea voyage, me lad, and don't imagine it will be for your health.' He gave one of his bellowing laughs and if ever I felt hatred for anyone I did for him then. But so far as I was concerned he had me where he wanted me. All I could do was desperately to think of a way of escaping and there didn't seem to be any.

As we came outside I saw that it was a tiny dilapidated cottage which we had been in. There was a straggling, unkempt front garden across which a weed-grown path brought us to a roadway which was scarcely more than a track and where a big station-wagon waited. Putting the signalling lamp on to the back seat, he pushed me in beside him. The track gave on to a narrow road which was equally unfrequented from its appearance, for a ridge of grass grew down its centre. It was, in fact, all but a cliff path, for from its farther side quite clearly now the sound of the sea came up from far below.

We drove for only a few minutes before he brought the big van to a standstill. Getting out, he pointed to where a gap in the cliff top was illuminated in the headlights. From it a narrow, twisting path led steeply downwards. From what I could see, its surface after the recent rain looked slippery and treacherous.

'Get going,' he said, indicating the path.

The germ of an idea was beginning to form in my mind.

'How do you think I can get down there with my hands tied behind my back?' I said. 'I'm groggy enough as it is with that belt over the head you gave me. If you want me down there you'll either have to carry me or untie me.'

He paused for a bit in thought, giving me a hard, calculating look before at last saying, 'No tricks, mind. Remember I've got a gun. All right, then. Turn around.'

Doing as I was told, I felt his hands on the cords round my wrists. He swore as he struggled with the knots and then I heard the click of a knife opening. It sliced through the cords, they fell away and my hands were free. His hands would be busy with the knife. It would take him a bit to get at the gun. I kicked out blindly backwards.

I was lucky. The heel of my shoe caught him squarely on the shin. There was a howl of rage and his hands fell away. Then I ran.

I had no idea where I was going. All I knew was that it was my one chance to get away and at the back of my mind was the idea that if I could get into those little fields in the darkness I might throw off pursuit.

Down the road I pelted, telling myself again it would take him a few moments to get the gun out and every yard I covered was a bonus to throw off his aim. A corner was coming up which made things hard for him, too. A shot rang out but he was firing wild and I didn't even hear the bullet's passing. Then I was round the corner and out of his sight. The road twisted again through another corner which would confuse him more. But on one side of me was the cliff edge guarded only by a flimsy and broken-down wire fence, on the other was a tall, impenetrable bank which held out no opportunity for me to reach the fields beyond. Behind me I heard a car start up and caught the flash of headlights. Desperately I tried to put on speed. The bank beside me was unbroken by gap or gateway. The car revved up and the headlights illuminated the corner. In a minute or two I'd be pinned in those lights like a fly on a wall. My breath was beginning to come in gasps. The roar of the engine came nearer and the lights became brighter. To the right the bank had given way to a high loose-stone wall.

Think, I told myself in desperation, use what the Colonel called your brains, if they're ever to help you the time is now. Another shot rang out and the lights closed in. Something sang overhead, near this time. I'd never been shot at before and found that it concentrates the mind wonderfully. He must be shooting out of the driver's window and was unlikely to make good practice. It would be more to frighten me than anything else, since a hit-and-run accident would suit his purpose better than a body with a bullet in it. And if he was shooting he must have only one hand on the wheel. I had to throw him off somehow and I hadn't much time. Suddenly I saw on my right that the top of the wall was broken where stones had fallen. There must be some sort of grip and foothold there. I knew I had to wait for the last instant rather like a matador waiting the rush of the bull in the corrida. It came. I jumped for the wall.

He swerved after me to catch me in mid-air and he damn nearly did it. I thought I felt the wind of the big van missing me by inches. My foot hit a crevice and further up an out-jutting stone held my hand. He was a bare second too late and what's more he overdid it. His nearside front wheel and wing hit the stones with a crash which shook the whole wall.

As I pulled myself up gasping for breath and with my heart banging away, I turned to look. And then I saw that a new element had come on the scene. There was another car, headlights blazing, bearing down on the van. Those lights behind him must have been enough to throw off his aim as he went for me. He must have been half-blinded by them. As it was, I saw him put up his free hand as if in protection from them. I guessed that it was that which caused the providential few inches by which he had missed me.

Then I saw him fighting the wheel of the big van, seeking to regain control as it slewed across the road from the impact with the wall. The muddied surface of the road afforded little grip and the car behind was bearing remorselessly down on him. The whole scene was illuminated in its headlights. The van straightened itself for a second and then, as if possessed of a life of its own, it plunged forward. It smashed the flimsy fence guarding the cliff as if it was paper. Then it was over the edge into the abyss and out into nothingness. A crash like a thousand tin cans being crushed marked its descent. There followed a moment of silence and then a terrible splash.

The car behind had pulled up, its lights shining on the gap in the fence. As I climbed down the driver's door opened and a figure stepped out. It was Denzil Colton. 'The 7th Cavalry have arrived,' he said.

'How the hell did you get here?' I said.

'Ask her, she'll tell you,' was his reply.

Looking in, I saw Jo sitting rigid, very white-faced in the passenger seat. 'Well, we made it,' she said between trembling lips. 'Are you all right?'

'Just about, thanks to you both,' I said. 'It was a damn near-run thing. How about you?'

'Before we get into explanations,' Denzil's voice broke in, 'I think we'd better take a look.'

Together we walked to the gap in the fence. Far, far below, we could see the water hard up against the base of the cliffs. Of van and occupant there was no sign. 'Sunk without trace,' Denzil said coolly. 'Very nasty accident. Car went out of control. Well, well.'

'And there'll be no landing of arms tonight,' I said. 'He took the signalling lamp with him.'

'We'd better not hang about here, just the same,' Denzil said. 'And you can thank Jo for us coming along like the 7th Cavalry. If we did anything, that is to say.'

'I think you saved my life,' I said. 'He meant having me one way or another.'

In the car going back they told me how they came to be there. Jo, it appeared, had been increasingly worried about me and what she considered, when she thought about it, was her desertion of me. On her own initiative she had got in touch with Denzil to see if he would help. Always ready for a piece of the action, Denzil said he would follow my tracks to Ireland and this time Jo had insisted on accompanying him. They had arrived in Amory's box not long after I had been spirited away. Amory, to use Jo's expression, was in a state of nerves or, as Denzil put it, he had the breeze up vertically, 'And I added a bit to make it a gale and he sang like a canary.'

I didn't inquire what his methods of persuasion had been. It didn't take much, I knew now, to frighten Amory, especially when he knew that he was into something far out of his depth. He had had quite an afternoon, too, with its ups and downs—victory in a big race and then terror lurking behind it. He'd have talked, all right.

'So he told all,' I said.

'Even to the exact location of the arms drop,' Denzil said happily. 'I think he'd have given us a map if he'd got one.'

'I told him straight when they had me cornered in the box,' I said. 'Betrayal is his business.' I looked at Jo as I said it.

'I still won't have too much said against him,' Jo said. 'After all, what he told us took us to you. All right, maybe he did let everyone down but he was caught in a web not of his own making and he didn't know how to get out. I still like him if you want to know and I think it was because of me he told us where you were and not Denzil's coming the heavy.'

'Perhaps,' I said and wondered not for the first time about women.

Denzil laughed as he trod on the accelerator and sent the car flying along the lonely, empty roads.

'I wonder what will happen to him now,' she said.

We had not long to wait to find out.

Two days later we were in the flat and I was looking through the morning papers. A black headline tucked away in a corner caught my eye. DEATH OF A LEADING RACE-HORSE OWNER, it said. I read on.

> Mr Amory Brayne, owner of this year's Irish Derby winner Midsummer Day, was found dead in his residence, Craddockscourt Castle, County Kilderry. An empty bottle of barbiturate tablets was at his bedside. Foul play is not suspected.
>
> Obituary page 13.

In silence I passed the paper to Jo, indicating the passage. In silence she read it. Then she handed the paper back to me.

'Poor Amory,' she said, and, looking at her, I saw that her eyes were moist.

We sat like that for a few moments and then she said firmly, 'I'm going to the funeral.'

'If you go, I go too,' I said, though I could not feel it in my heart to weep salt tears into my breakfast coffee over the demise of Amory Brayne. I turned to the death notices. It was there all right. 'At his residence, Craddockscourt Castle, County Kilderry. Funeral arrangements later,' it went on to say.

'Later' turned out to be two days. He was to be buried from Craddockscourt, service in the local church, interment afterwards in the adjoining cemetery. We caught the morning flight to Cork and hired a car at the airport. It seemed strange not to be driving straight to Pollardstown and even stranger when we passed the entrance without turning in. The gates, I noticed, had been freshly painted, the pillars cleaned and stone polished and they shone as they had never done in my memory, nor living memory either, for that matter.

The little church was packed, all the notabilities of the county, what was left of them, were there and representatives from the racing world on both sides of the water. We found seats and I let my thoughts stray, pondering over all that had happened, how in an odd way the wheel had turned full circle and I had found myself and, more important, had found Jo and we had found each other. I stole a look at her. She was sitting staring at one of the memorials on the walls. It was to her great-grandfather whose *folie de grandeur* had begun the fall of her family and it was as elaborate as his ideas and his buildings. I wondered then what thoughts were passing through her head—was the sadness of being here, near it, and yet farther away than ever from Pollardstown, gripping her? I thought, too, of the anomaly of Amory Brayne. He had come out of nowhere, gained everything the world he wanted could offer, and now he had gone no one knew whither, destroyed despite all he had by his own inner weaknesses and frailties. Then I gave myself a mental shrug and put such thoughts away from me, for the service was ending and we were trooping out of the church.

As we were leaving the graveside after making our condolences to Camilla, Paul Davey came up to us.

'I was hoping you'd be here,' he said to Jo after he had greeted us, 'for I didn't know where to contact you. Amory left a sealed packet in my office with a note to say it was only to be opened in your presence. How are you fixed for this afternoon? Can you come in?'

Jo said she could and that I would come too and we followed his car back to Kilderry. Once in his office, he summoned his clerk to 'get that sealed package Mr Brayne left in', from the strongroom.

'What on earth can it be?' Jo said to him.

'I'm afraid I have as little idea as you have,' Davey said. 'Mysteries seem to abound where your family are concerned.' He smiled as he said it and in a few minutes the clerk was back.

It was a large, buff envelope, foolscap size, folded twice. Davey took it and, with a heavy paper knife, souvenir of some trip abroad, slit one side. Within was another envelope coloured blue. Taking this out, he regarded it with something like distaste. 'It's a homemade codicil to his will,' he said. 'You can buy these forms in any stationers. I only hope . . .' In turn he slit this envelope and took out the enclosure. Rapidly scanning its contents, he breathed what appeared to be a sigh of relief and looked up. 'We're always terrified of homemade wills,' he said. 'God knows we make enough mistakes ourselves, but laymen—' He raised his eyes to the ceiling. 'However,' he went on, 'this looks all right. He seems to have known what he was doing. It's perfectly executed, witnessed and attested so far as I can see.'

'Yes,' I said, 'but what's in it? What has it to do with us, with Jo, I mean.'

He read it again and then looked up at Jo. 'He has left you Pollardstown and everything on it,' he said quietly.

There was silence between the three of us broken only by Jo's sudden intake of breath. 'It's unbelievable,' she said. 'Is it, will it—?'

'I know what you are going to say,' Paul Davey said. 'Will it, as the country people say, "stand law"? I see no reason why not. Here it is, read it for yourself.' He passed the sheet of paper across the desk to her and she beckoned to me to read it with her.

There it was in black and white though the writing, I noticed, was shaky enough: *I leave the house and lands of Pollardstown, County Kilderry, and all stock which may be thereon at the time of my death to Joanna (Jo) Manners formerly of Pollardstown House as some small amends for the wrongs to her and her family to which I was a party.*

'But . . . but . . .' she said, 'what about the sale and the purchase money?'

'You keep that, of course,' Davey said. 'The contract is enforceable and he had gone into possession.'

'I'm still pinching myself to make myself believe it's true,' she said when we were back in the street. 'And I think I feel quite faint.'

'There's only one remedy for that,' I said.

In five minutes we were in the snug where I had met Jack Manley and an open bottle of champagne was on the table before us. 'Pollardstown,' she said. 'Free of debt and with the money to run it. Oh, Charles, what made him do it?'

'He wanted to wipe the slate clean as best he could,' I said. 'And he's done it or nearly, give him that.'

'Pollardstown,' she said again. 'And you'll come too, won't you, Charles?'

She was asking me. I was right. The wheel had come full circle. I was not only wanted; I was needed. That snipe bog they could shoot snipe off—me—was banished forever. I filled her glass and pushed it towards her. As she took it our hands touched and our eyes met. 'Try to stop me,' I said.